U0038519

Diane's Diary

黛安的日記

三民書局

May, 31

Dad came home with exciting news tonight. His company is transferring him to America. We'll all be going with him. Next year, when school starts I'll be studying in an American school. All my classmates will be Americans. Of course, Mom is excited too, but she also worries. Dad tells her not to worry, but it's no use. Mom is a practical* person. Practical people worry too much. She worries about what kind of school I'll go to. She worries whether my English will be good enough. She worries about finding a nice house. "Finding a house won't be a problem," Dad says. "Let's think now about what we'll need to take with us." I don't think about those things. I'm too excited. After dinner we watched an American program on television. It seemed different than before. I guess that's because we're going there. I know I'm going to have trouble sleeping tonight.*

June, 1

Well, I was right. I didn't sleep well. In fact, I don't think anybody slept well last night, not even my brother. Usually nothing ever wakes him. Mom says the house could catch on fire and he'd sleep right through it. I could hear my parents talking, but not what they were saying. Suddenly* I could hear them clearly. My father was saying, "Maybe I'd better go to America alone." Mom asked, "Who'll take care of you." And Dad replied*, "Maybe just the two of us should go together and leave the children here." Mom thought about this for a while and said, "Yes, we could leave them with your parents." When I heard this I cried out, "No, no, don't leave me here. Take me with you." I opened my eyes and found out it was just a bad dream. I was so happy. Then I saw a shadow* at my bedroom door. It was my brother, Peter. "What do you want?" I asked. Peter said, "You were screaming*. You woke me up." And I always thought he slept like a pig. "Well, I'm sorry," I said. "Go back to bed." What a night! Even my brother couldn't sleep.*

June, 2

Today is Sunday. My uncle and his wife came over for lunch. Of course the only thing we talked about was our coming move to America. My aunt is very supportive. She thinks it's a wonderful opportunity*. She believes travel is good for everyone, especially for young people. "The younger they are, the more they'll get out of it," she says. "When I was a university* student I spent one summer studying in England. I met many interesting friends and traveled all over England. I even made a short trip to Europe." She talked happily about her summer of travel. "After I graduated* from the university I went to work. Then I got married. There were no more opportunities for travel. In looking back, my summer in England was the happiest time of my life." She sighed*. I looked at my uncle. Whenever my aunt talks like this, my uncle never smiles.*

June
July
August
September

June, 3

I want to say something about my uncle. He's a strange guy. Of course I love him, but let's face it, he's got some weird ideas. He's my mother's older brother. Like my mother, he also worries. It seems everyone in their family worries. But with my uncle it's more than just worry. He can never see the bright side of things. He believes terrible things will happen to us in America. His words made my mother worry even more. The trouble is my uncle has never traveled abroad. He thinks it's a waste of money. But I think he is just jealous. He doesn't trust foreigners. Whenever there's an American movie on television, he'll say, "Look how those foreigners act. They're all really crazy." After lunch he told my parents, "You'll lose your daughter. She'll marry a foreigner and you'll never see her again." Even my mother smiled when he said that. "I don't think we'll have to worry about that," she said. "Don't forget Diane is only 9 years old." Like I said, my uncle is kind of weird.*

June, 4

The day for leaving is getting closer and closer. Dad's work keeps him busy, so Mom has to decide what we'll take and what we'll leave behind. At night, that's just about all they talk about. Suddenly it seems as if nothing else is important. I see my friends going about their usual lives and, even though I'm still here, I already feel different from them. They say they envy me, and they probably do. But in a way, I envy them, too. They would never understand this. At night, the idea of going away doesn't seem as exciting as it did at first. I can't help it. But I always feel brave and confident when the morning sun rises and I'm ready to face the future. I asked Peter if he feels uncomfortable about going. His reply was short and to the point: "Why? We'll all be together. We'll meet new friends. Aunt Sally said that America is a heaven* for kids. What are you worried about?" He's right. I'm becoming like Mom.*

June, 5

This afternoon I went to my aunt Sally's house. I wanted to hear more about what it's like to live abroad. Sometimes I think she's the only person I can talk with. She brought out her photo albums and showed me the pictures from her year in England. I've seen them hundreds of times, but today they seemed different than before. That's because I was looking at them through different eyes. The buildings looked more beautiful. The people seemed different. I looked closely. I wondered if this is what people from outer space might look like. Today I said to my aunt, "It's hard to believe I'll be going to this kind of place." "You won't," my aunt said. "These pictures were taken in England. You're going to America. There's a big difference." I told her I don't understand. "They all speak English," I said. "How can they be different?" My aunt only smiled. "When you're old enough to travel, You'll find out for yourself." "Hey," I thought, "I came here for some quick answers. But now I'm going home with more questions!"*

June, 6

This morning Mom told us workmen will be arriving tomorrow to pack everything for shipping. She said the whole house will be a mess* and she doesn't want us around. She says we'll be in the way*. "But where will we go?" I wailed*. I felt like crying. It seems our whole world is gradually* being turned upside down. My brother called me a crybaby. But I know he was just pretending* to be cool. Down inside he's just as worried as I am, but won't show it. Mom told us we'll be staying with our grandparents until it's time to go. When she said this, my brother's eyes got real big. He didn't look so cool anymore. He looked scared. He looked over at me and I could tell we were both thinking the same thing. Our grandparents live in the country. Maybe Mom and Dad were really going to America by themselves. Maybe this was just a way to get rid of* us? Maybe they're going to go by themselves and leave us behind?*

September August July June

June, 7

The workmen rang our bell at exactly* 8:00 a.m. They came loudly into our apartment and got to work with hammer and saw*, making the wooden crates*. Bang, bang, bang. It was really noisy. In no time at all our house looked like a battle field*. Luckily, we had packed our things last night. Just as we were going out the door, I felt very sad as I looked around at the mess in my bedroom. Hopefully, I asked Mom if I should stay and help. She just patted* me on the head and told me to hurry up. But I know she understood how I felt. Aunt Sally had to take us to my grandparents'* because Mom was too busy. When the big engine rumbled* into the station we climbed aboard and took our seats. Aunt Sally smiled at us kindly. "Cheer up! You both look like you're going to prison*! You're going to have a great time." Then we started to move. Buildings flashed* by as we picked up speed. I was too sad to notice anything. I missed my bedroom. Above all, I missed Mom and Dad. "Aunt Sally," I asked fearfully. "They won't go to America without us, will they?"

June, 8

We arrived late in the afternoon. Our uncle A-yi, Dad's older brother, came to the train station to pick us up. He usually rides a motorcycle, but because there were so many of us, we took a bus to their village. It's quite far and the ride takes nearly an hour. After we got off the bus, we still had to take a local taxi to get to my grandparent's farm. The farm is located in the foothills* and is quite isolated*. By the time we arrived it was already getting dark. The family had waited for us so we could all eat dinner together. I was starving*. After dinner Peter and I watched television. I could tell from the way my grandparents talked, they don't think the way Taipei people do. They weren't sure going to a foreign country was such a good idea. "So far away," they said. "So dangerous," others said. Outside stars were shining in a clear sky. I've never seen so many stars in Taipei. I already felt like I was in a foreign land. I was so tired I fell asleep on the sofa.*

June
July
August
September

June, 9

This morning the sun shining in my face woke me up. There was no one around. I was lying in a strange bed. Where was I? I could hear birds singing. This seemed strange because I never hear birds in Taipei. Maybe this was a dream? I wasn't scared, but I was puzzled. Slowly, yesterday's events came back to me. The train ride from Taipei. My grandparents. I remembered sitting on the sofa. After that, nothing. Somebody must have carried me to this bed when I fell asleep. Where was Aunt Sally? Where was Peter? I got up and dressed quickly. When I came into the living room, my grandmother asked, "Are you hungry?" To tell the truth, I was very hungry, but I could hear children playing outside and I wanted to see what they were doing. My cousins must have come over. I wanted to hurry out and join them. I could hear Peter's voice. I could tell they were having fun. Who needs to eat? I'd already wasted too much time. I wanted to get outside and join them. I didn't want to wait a single minute!

June, 10

Today the weather was very hot. Peter said our cousin Liang-sung was going to take us somewhere. Cousin Liang-sung is my brother's best friend. Whenever we're in the country, if you see Liang-sung you can be sure Peter is near by. "Let's go catch shrimps," Liang-sung said, and off we went. We followed him with excitement. He led us to a clear stream, not far away, where there are lots of shrimps. On the way, we met several of his friends. There aren't many houses in this area, but there sure are lots of children. Liang-sung invited every one we met to come along. No one refused. They knew we are from Taipei and they were very curious about us. I felt a bit embarrassed because Peter and I were the only ones wearing shoes. The others were all barefoot*. I tried to take my shoes off, but the pebbles* on the path were so hot, they burned my feet. I had to put them back on. When we reached the stream, I quickly put my feet in the water and it felt so good. Do you know shrimps always jump back when you try to catch them? I didn't. But now I do.*

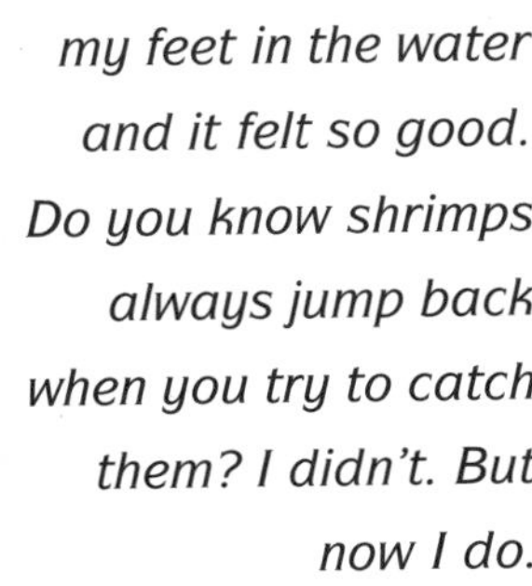

June
July
August
September

June, 11

We had some real excitement today. Grandmother found a snake coiled* under one of the bamboo* chairs in the living room. My grandparents' house sits on a mountain-side. During the summer, snakes are always a problem. High ceilings keep the house cool even on the hottest day. Unfortunately*, snakes like a cool house. They will crawl* in to escape* the heat. Today when we were playing in front of the house we suddenly heard my grandmother shout. We rushed inside and I couldn't believe my eyes! A huge and evil-looking snake was coiled under one of the chairs. Grandfather removed it from the house. I asked him why he didn't kill it. He said, "Snakes always have a mate*. If you kill one, the other will come looking for it. We don't need another snake in the house." Afterwards I told Grandmother I was glad she was the one who found the snake. "If it had been me," I said, "I would have had a heart attack*." "Don't be silly," Grandmother said, "Children don't have heart attacks." Oh-oh. I think I'm going to have trouble sleeping tonight.

June, 12

I was right. Last night it took me a long time to fall asleep. I kept hearing strange sounds. Snake sounds. I was sure they were coming from right under my bed! I could imagine a snake coiled right below me, waiting to bite me when I stepped down. What if it crawled up on my bed? I covered myself from head to toe with the blanket. Even though the night was warm, it made me feel safe. When I woke up in the morning, I peeked over the edge* of the bed first to make sure there was no snake waiting for me. When I told my grandfather, he told me not to worry. "Snakes are night hunters," he said. "The nights are cool so that's when they go hunting. They're not interested in houses at night. But in the day, they sometimes crawl into houses to escape from the heat." That made me feel a little better. Every night we bring our bamboo chairs outside. We sit in the dark talking and looking up at the stars. It's cool out there. I fell asleep under the night sky.*

June
July
August
September

June, 13

This morning, Liang-sung and his sister Siao-ping took us to hunt for snails. Liang-sung's job is to take care of their ducks. They told us ducks like to eat snails and they asked us to come along and help. Snails are found near places that are wet and cool. These are also the same kind of places snakes like, so we had to be careful. Liang-sung had a stick with him. He first beat the grass to scare away the snakes. Then we went in and started gathering snails. Peter and I couldn't see them, but Liang-sung and Siao-ping showed us where to look. We placed all the snails in a bag and went back to my cousin's house. Liang-sung took a large kitchen knife and whack, whack! crushed all the snails into a gooey* mess. It was really disgusting*. But I guess if you're a duck it tastes good. On the way home a heavy rain started. Liang-sung quickly picked some large leaves for us to cover our heads with. We held the stalks* and used our leaves as umbrellas. When we got home, we were all wet. I've never had so much fun in the rain before.*

June, 14

Something happened today that was really funny. Even now, when I think about it, I start laughing again. Peter disappeared today. Sounds mysterious, doesn't it? We couldn't find him for about half an hour. He was chasing Liang-sung and the two of them ran up the slope* behind the house, giggling* and laughing. Pretty soon Liang-sung came back, alone. "Where's Peter?" Siao-ping and I asked. "He was right behind me," Liang-sung said. We waited and waited, but there was no sign of Peter. "He's probably hiding out there," Liang-sung said, but I didn't think so. Where could he be? We started looking for him. We searched behind the house. We called his name. No answer. Then we heard a faint cry, "Help, help! I'm over here!" We ran over, and there he was. He had fallen into the cesspool*! We all burst out laughing. Even my brother. He couldn't get out, so we had to help pull him up. He was covered with filth*. My grandmother had to use a hose* to wash it off. It's so much fun here. I never want to leave.*

September August July June

June, 15

Tonight my uncle said he had to buy some things from the store. He told me to come along with him. It's a 20-minute walk. I think I ought to* first say something about my uncle. Even though my uncle is 20 years old, he still has a boy's heart. When we were walking back, he suddenly said, "Wait! I see a ghost under that tree!" I screamed. If you've ever been in the country at night and someone tells you he sees a ghost, you'll know how scared I was. I hid my face. I didn't want to look. Would you? My uncle really sounded scared when he said, "There's another one in front of us and one more coming up from behind!" "Let's run," he shouted. He grabbed* my hand and we started to run. I screamed all the way. I was sure that ghost would grab me any minute. When we got home my uncle fell down on the ground, laughing. It had been a joke. But it was a good joke, and I wasn't mad. Not at all. My uncle had really sounded scared out there in the dark. He would have made a good movie star. I'm having so much fun here! Who else is lucky enough to have an uncle who's so much fun?

June, 16

This morning Grandfather told us we will be leaving tomorrow. This is our last day. After dinner my uncle said, "Tonight is special. Let's play with firecrackers." "Yes, yes, let's do it!" we all shouted. We crowded around him when he came out. My uncle placed a firecracker on the ground and lit it. It exploded* with a loud bang. We all cheered. He then put one under a can and lit it. The can flew into the air. "Uncle, let me light one." My cousins were getting restless. But my uncle was looking around for other things to blow up. He looked towards the cat. The cat jumped and was gone, quick as lightning. The dog eyed my uncle nervously and wagged* its tail. "Please, Uncle, let us try," Peter begged*. "You kids are too small. You might get hurt." Then we understood. My uncle was having so much fun he didn't want to stop. I feel I've lived here all my life. Taipei seems so far away. And America? Gosh, sounds like another planet*.*

June, 17

Time to go. One of my uncles is taking us to the airport. I want to see Mom and Dad again, but I hate to leave my grandparents. I almost couldn't get my shoes on this morning. I've been running around barefoot so much my shoes feel uncomfortable. They're too tight. Our cousins and some other children came to say goodbye. They were all very quiet. None of the usual loud plans for the day's activity. Cousin Liang-sung gave me a present. "So you'll remember us," he said. It was a grasshopper he had fashioned* from a leaf. Can life in America be as exciting as life here in the country? No cousins, no fun-loving uncle. No snakes, no snails, no ducks. As we walked out, towards the road, I turned to look back. They were all standing there, waving. I'll miss my grandmother. As soon as we got on the bus, Peter fell asleep. Just like him. No feelings. Why does the ride to the CKS International Airport take so long?*

June, 18

I'm writing this on the plane. I don't know what time it is. I don't know if it's still today or already tomorrow. We took off a long time ago, but it's still dark outside. When we arrived at the airport Mom and Dad were waiting out in front to meet us. We were so happy to see them. We must have arrived a little late because they both looked a little worried. As soon as we got there, we all went upstairs. We passed through a gate where some people in uniform were checking passports. Then a little further on someone checked the bags we were carrying. When we got to the waiting room, people were already getting on the plane. Peter said I could have the window seat for the first part of the trip. Mom is sitting in the middle, next to me. Suddenly there was a loud roar* and a burst of power as the plane rushed forward and up into the sky. I looked down into the dark from the window. I could see tiny points of light. I wondered if one of them was my grandparents' home.*

June July August September

June, 19

I just woke up. I don't know what day this is, or where I am. We're somewhere in the sky. Bright sunlight is coming in through the windows. My grandparents' house and my cousins seem so far away. Peter said I could have the window seat when we took off, but he said I have to give it back when we land. Now I understand why. There's nothing to see. Just a wide carpet of clouds. I feel cheated. Mom says we're over the ocean. I would have liked to see the water or maybe a boat, but there's nothing. Mom and Dad don't look so good in the early morning. I don't know why, but they look different. They're the same, but not the same. Maybe they didn't sleep so well. Neither did I. But nothing bothers* Peter. As usual, he's still sound asleep. When they announced* we were approaching* San Francisco, Peter made me give up the window seat. As we flew in over the California coast line, I could just see a glimpse* of green mountains. Now we're getting ready to land. I've got to stop writing.

June, 19

[Same day, 11:30 p.m.]

Just a little time to write down some things before I turn off the light. It's been a busy night. After the plane pulled up at the gate, all the passengers started putting on their coats and taking bags down from overhead lockers. Before, everyone had been sleeping or looking bored. Now they were suddenly all very busy. When the plane door opened, everyone started walking very fast. Some people were almost running. I asked Dad why. He said maybe they had someone waiting for them outside. We had to wait in a long line to have our passports checked. The immigration* officer didn't look very friendly. He asked a few questions and stamped our passports. We picked up our suitcases* and entered the greeting area. Mr. Johnson from my father's office was there to meet us. He went to get the car while we waited outside the front entrance. It was dark by now and the air was chilly*. It felt strangely exciting. Then Mr. Johnson drove up and we got in the car. We were in America.*

June
July
August
September

June, 20

Our first morning in America. When I woke up, Dad had already gone to the office. I got up from the soft bed, walked across the soft carpet and opened the curtains. Outside, 20 stories* down, lay San Francisco. I couldn't get over how lovely it looked in the clear sunlight. I could see the bay* and the bridge and the hills beyond. It was more beautiful than I had imagined! Peter and I were so excited we were jumping around the room, telling Mom to hurry up. San Francisco was waiting for us! When we stepped into the hall, the soft carpets and the empty corridor* were too big a temptation*. Peter and I raced down the corridor to see who could press the elevator button* first. Mom called out sharply*, "Behave yourselves! If the manager sees you running around like this we'll get thrown out." Outside in the air and sunshine, we walked for a while but soon felt very tired. I couldn't understand it. Mom told us jet lag* made us feel that way. Our bodies were still on Taiwan time, where it was now about 2:00 a.m. Our bodies were telling us they wanted to sleep.

June, 21

Today is Sunday. This morning Dad said we'll be leaving San Francisco after dinner and driving to a town in central California. That will be our home for the coming year. We checked out of our rooms at noon and left our bags with the hotel. Even though Sunday is a day off in America, Dad still had many things to do before we left. He said he would meet us back at the hotel at 5:30. After he left, the three of us, Mom, Peter and I, stood outside the hotel and discussed where to go. Every direction looked inviting. On one side, California Street descends* towards Chinatown, but we weren't interested in seeing Chinatown. We'd just arrived from Taiwan. We wanted to see something different, so we headed off for Union Square.*

When we got to the corner of Powell St. we stopped in surprise. We never thought it would be so steep!*

When we got back to the hotel, Dad was waiting for us and we had dinner before setting off. Everyone was unusually quiet during the meal. Jet lag is still affecting all of us.

June September August July June

June, 22

This morning Peter and I took a short walk before breakfast. We're staying in a small hotel near the train station. The hotel is different than the one in San Francisco, which was very elegant, but this one is very neat* and has a friendly feeling. Just like this town. We arrived quite late last night. During the ride I discovered something: America is really BIG! You have to see it to understand. The Pacific Ocean* is big, too, but planes fly so high you don't feel it. On our map, this town is only about 2 inches away from San Francisco. "A short trip," I thought. But in a car, it took us hours to get here! I fell asleep soon after we started out. When I woke up, we still hadn't arrived. We drove on and on through empty darkness. No road signs, no other cars, just miles and miles of darkness in every direction. Occasionally there was a tiny light in the distance, probably a lonely farm house. Then more miles of darkness. I wanted to tell Dad how I felt, but I was too tired. Mom says they had trouble waking me up after we arrived.*

June, 23

Today we're going house-hunting. Dad made an appointment yesterday with a real estate* agent*. "We want to find a house," he said, "and we don't want to waste time." Dad says it's not good for children to be living in hotels. I know Peter likes staying in a hotel. That way he doesn't have to clean his room. I'm like Dad. I want to get settled down* quickly. I want my own room. I want all my own things around me. After breakfast, the real estate agent met us in the hotel lobby*. Her name is Mrs. Barnes. Dad had already explained what kind of house we needed. Mrs. Barnes had prepared a list of several homes she thought we might like. Mrs. Barnes had her own car and of course we have our rental car, but neither car was big enough for all of us. "Does anyone want to ride with me?" Mrs. Barnes asked, and Mom said she would. I would have liked to ride with her, because she seems so nice, but I only know a few words of English. What if she had started talking to me! I would have died of embarrassment.*

June, 24

Two whole days of house-hunting. All of them are so nice, just like the homes in American movies. The kids in American movies always seem to live in nice homes. And soon we will, too. Mom and Peter and I can't decide which one is best. Dad hasn't said anything. One thing about Dad. When he has to make a decision, he does it right away. Making a decision is no problem for him. And he always seems to make the right decision, too. That's probably why he has such an important job in his company. Dad's not one of those people who needs to think things over for several days. Mom is a little different. Peter takes after Dad, but sometimes he's also like Mom. I'm more like Mom. All the houses we looked at had nice yards, big kitchens, two-car garages and at least 3 bedrooms. The only difference seemed to be in size. Some had bigger yards, others had more bedrooms. I love looking at these beautiful homes. I'm looking forward to* tomorrow.*

June, 25

At breakfast this morning Dad told us, "No more house-hunting. We've seen enough." Peter and I were silent, waiting. "Your Mom and I talked it over last night and we've decided the house on McDaniel Avenue is the best." McDaniel Avenue? Peter and I only remember what places and things look like. Names don't mean anything to us. We can't tell one English name from the other. After breakfast, we went to the real estate office and Dad signed the rental lease*. Then Mrs. Barnes gave us the keys and we drove off to our new home. But today, we looked at it with different eyes. Now it was ours, at least for a year, and that makes a difference in how you see things. It looked even better than before. The house is near the sidewalk, so the front yard is small, but the backyard is deep and wide. It has a large lawn*, bordered* by trees and shrubs*. Best of all, there is a swimming pool! Can you imagine it? Our own swimming pool! This is going to be the happiest summer of my entire* life!*

June

July

August

September

June, 26

We checked out of the hotel and moved into our new home this morning. The house is what Americans call "partially furnished*." That means it has furniture, a washing machine, refrigerator and stove, but no linen*. So we spent the morning buying sheets, blankets, pillowcases* and towels. Afterwards we went to the market to buy soap and bathroom articles*. I thought we would shop for food, but Dad said, "No, there were other things we had to do first." After lunch we drove Mom home. She wanted to make the beds* and start putting the house in order. Dad then drove to a very large park. It was much larger than anything in Taipei. Grass and trees, all clean and well-kept, stretching* for blocks under a blue sky! Just looking at it made me want to take off my shoes and run, or chase Peter, or just lie on the grass. We entered a low building among some trees. Dad spoke to a young woman behind a desk. She looked over and smiled at me. Her eyes were kind and twinkling*. I liked her the minute our eyes met.*

June, 27

This morning Mom told us, "Today we're going to the supermarket and shop for food. From now on we're going to eat at home." "Great," I thought, "Now I'll see the inside of an American supermarket." When we got there Peter said, "Wow, Mom, this place is huge!" There were piles of fresh vegetables and fruits. I could only recognize a few of them. There were rows and rows of things I'd never seen in Taipei. The store was so big we lost Peter a couple of times. He wandered* off by himself and we couldn't find him. We bought a "wok*," too. "I don't know how to cook with those flat American pans," Mom said. "If I have to use American pans, we might starve to death." That night we had our very first home-cooked meal in America. To tell the truth, it didn't taste too good. Mom said she didn't know how to control the heat on our electric stove. As a result she burned the fish. But we didn't mind. In fact, we all laughed. After a week of hotel and restaurant food that burned fish tasted delicious.*

September August July June

June, 28

Sunday. Dad started the morning off with some bad news. He has signed us up for summer camp. That's what he was doing at the park. Peter looked at me and I knew what he was thinking. Neither of us can speak more than a few words of English. Peter looked worried and I'm sure I did too. Anyhow, I sure FELT worried. Dad smiled when he saw our expressions. "Cheer up," he said. "Don't look so sad. You're going to be with other kids. You're going to have fun. The girl I was talking to on Friday is the program director. She's a student at the university. She said language won't be a problem. She said kids your age learn very fast, and that's true. I'll bet* by the time school starts in September, the two of you will be pretty good." I didn't say anything. I know he meant well and was trying to encourage* us. In my heart I didn't believe him. The only English I know is "Hi!" and "Hello?" and Mom tells me even my "hello?" doesn't sound right. She says it sounds like "ha-lou."*

June, 29

I'm so tired I can hardly move. Today was the first day of summer camp. My whole body aches from games and activities. And from being nervous, too. The nice lady we saw on Friday took us to our classrooms. Because Peter is older, he's in a different group. When Peter went into his room, I felt kind of alone. I could hear kids laughing and talking in nearby classrooms. Summer camp has already been going for a week, so the children all know one another. My teacher said, "C'mon, Diane, let's meet the other kids." When we walked in, everyone turned to look. I felt very shy. "We have a new friend today," the teacher said. "Diane's family just moved to town last week. Let's all welcome her." All the kids smiled and called out, "Hi, Diane!" They were very nice to me, but I can't talk to them and I don't understand what's being said. Luckily, today's activities were simple. I just followed the other kids. Even then I made mistakes. How will I ever get through* tomorrow?*

June, 30

In the morning the teacher gave us an art project. It was easy, and kind of fun, too. The girl sitting next to me did everything slowly so I could follow her. She calls me Diane, but I don't know enough English to ask her name. All I can do is smile. After lunch, the class played some games, but I couldn't understand what we were supposed to* do. The teacher was very nice to me. He said, "Diane, let's go over here and sit down. You and I can talk while the others play." We sat on the grass and he asked me about my family. Simple questions. Did I have any brothers or sisters? I could only answer either "yes" or "no." I think he asked me what kind of work my father did, but I'm not sure. It must have been boring to talk with someone who can't answer. When it was time to go home, he spoke to me again. I smiled and said, "O.K." I hope that was the right thing to do. Anyway, he nodded and said, "Good. See you tomorrow." I wonder what he said.
Oh well, it probably wasn't important.
I hope.

July, 1

This morning I noticed all the kids had bundles with them. I was the only person who didn't have one. This made me a little nervous. Then, after lunch the teacher said, "O.K., everybody, time to go swimming!" I didn't understand him, but that's what he must have said, because the kids all cheered and hurried out the door. I followed along behind. Some kids ran all the way. Close by, surrounded by trees, is an outdoor swimming pool. When we got there, the kids hurried into the dressing rooms to change. That's when I realized what those bundles were. They were swimsuits and towels. The teacher looked at me, but didn't say anything. That's what he had been trying to tell me yesterday. All the kids quickly jumped into the water, diving and splashing* and laughing. They were having a wonderful time. I lay back on a chair near the pool and looked up at the sky. It was clear and blue. It was a perfect day for swimming and I was the only person who didn't bring a swimsuit.*

June
July
August
September

July, 2

In a way, maybe it was a good thing I didn't have my swimsuit with me yesterday. I noticed the swimsuits the kids were wearing were different from mine. I can't explain how, but they're just different, both for boys and girls. Last night after I finished writing my diary, I dug my swimsuit out and looked at it. In Taiwan it had looked all right, but now it didn't look so good. The style was not quite right. The colors seemed too bright. The swimsuits at camp were all softer colors. I explained my problem to Mom. I know she thought it was wasteful, but she said she'd ask Dad. Dad understood. "Kids hate being different," he said. "And Peter and Diane already feel different because they don't speak English. If buying a new swimsuit helps her fit in a little better, then by all means* get her one." Nobody understands me like Dad. So today when I got home from camp, Mom and I went to the store to look at swimsuits. I chose one that I was sure would be just right. I can hardly wait to try it out.*

July, 3

We have four different instructors, or leaders. Two in the morning, and then two different ones in the afternoon. They are all quite young. Well, that's what Dad says. They all look pretty old to me. Every one of them has lived in this town since they were children. They even attended* this same summer program when they were our age. I think that's interesting. America is so big and it's so easy to travel around, but they like this town so much they've never moved away. Rusty is one of our afternoon leaders. He's the one who sat down and talked with me on Tuesday. These last two days he came over and talked with me for a minute, even though he knows I can't understand much English. He told me everyone calls him "Rusty" because when he was younger, his hair was reddish*, like the color of rust*. Rusty's a student at the university. He'll be a senior when school starts in the fall. After he graduates he is going to be a teacher. I hope when I start school here my new teacher will be as nice as Rusty.*

September August July June

July, 4

Finally! A day of rest. No need to worry about understanding what people are saying. No need to worry about doing the wrong thing. Today is the 4th of July, America's Independence Day. It's a holiday and Dad didn't have to go to work. Later in the morning, we drove over to the university mall. Mom wanted to do some shopping for the coming week. When we enrolled for camp, each one of us was given a T-shirt. The words "Summer Camp Fun" are written across the front. I saw a group of several girls wearing Summer Camp shirts, but I didn't recognize* any of them. They were from another class. Or were they? I couldn't tell. I was wearing my shirt too, and later, when the group passed by, they said "Hi," even though I didn't know them. "See." Dad said, "Pretty soon, you're going to have lots of new friends." I told him without any English, I would never be able to make any friends. Dad just smiled and said, "Just wait. You'll see what I mean."*

July, 5

I've been practicing swimming every day. When we first moved into this house, I could only dog-paddle. On Wednesday I discovered most of the other kids are pretty good swimmers. In fact, some of them are very good. I've made up my mind*. I'm going to learn how to swim. Not just swim, but swim well. I'll probably never learn to speak English, but with a swimming pool in the backyard, I can certainly* become a better swimmer. I started practicing the same day I bought my new swimsuit. Already I've improved. Not a lot, but some. Dad helped me tonight. Dad is an excellent swimmer. He told me to just relax*. "Think of the water as your friend," he said. "Work with it. Whatever you do, don't fight it." He showed me how to use my legs and push out into the center of the pool. When Dad isn't looking, Peter laughs at me. I can tell he'd like to duck* my head in the water, but he doesn't dare*. He knows I would scream. Besides, he's not so good himself. Another week and we'll see who ducks who.*

June July August September

July, 6

Every time we go shopping Peter and I never worry about paying. It has nothing to do with us. We just wander around while either Mom or Dad pays. I don't have any idea how to count American money. Neither does Peter. Tonight Dad took some coins from his pocket and placed them on the table. "We live in America now," he said, "so you must learn how to use American money. Can you tell me how much each of these coins is worth?" We looked closely, but of course didn't know. Dad picked up a copper coin and said, "This is a penny*. It's worth 1 cent." He then pointed to the smallest coin. "This is a 'dime*.' It's worth 10 cents." For the next hour we practiced identifying* pennies, nickels*, dimes and quarters*. At first, we were a little slow, but we soon caught on*. Finally, after testing us with some questions, Dad said, "O.K. On Sunday I'll take you to the Co-op* for practice. We'll see how well you use American money." Sunday is a long way off. I'm afraid I'll forget everything in the meantime*.*

July, 7

The first week of camp I was too shy to notice the other kids in my group. Now I'm a little more comfortable, but I still have trouble telling the other kids apart. In a way it's like learning to count American money, only harder. Coins are easy. Faces take more time. At least those in my class do. Today Myra, our teacher, told me to pass crayons* out to the other students. I took the crayons and went around the room, giving some to each person. When I came to the last row, I hesitated*. The first girl looked familiar*. I wasn't sure if I'd already given her crayons or not. There weren't any on her desk. I was uncertain. The girl smiled and said, "I'm Carol. You just gave some crayons to my sister." She pointed to a girl in the first row. Then she added, "Don't feel bad. Lots of people get us mixed up*." I smiled as I gave her the crayons, but down inside I was thinking, "What am I going to do? All the girls in this class look like sisters to me!" There are still seven more weeks of camp to go. I'll never make it.*

June
July
August
September

July, 8

Swimming with a bunch of other kids is certainly more fun than swimming by yourself. I like having my own pool to swim in, but it's not the same. At home it's quiet and peaceful, or at least it is when Peter's not around. Maybe it's because I always swim alone, in the evening. I've been practicing very hard. For me, swimming at home is more serious. The pool in our yard has never seemed as much fun as the Community* Center pool was today. The skies were just as clear as last week, but this time I had my new swimsuit on, and I jumped in the water with the rest of them. It was unbelievable*. The boys immediately* took over the deep end of the pool. They were chasing each other, diving in and climbing out of the pool. The girls played by themselves. Some were diving for a coin to see who could find it first. I recognized it as a quarter. I splashed around in the shallow* end with some other kids. Tonight I'm stiff* and tired. I'm so sunburned* it hurts to lie down. I really had fun today.*

July, 9

So far, the games in summer camp have been kind of hard. Hard for me, not for the rest of the class. They're hard because I don't speak English. But today we played a game where I didn't have to talk. It was fun to play and fun to watch. At first, when Myra told us we were going to practice writing our names, the kids were disappointed. "C'mon*, Myra," they complained. "That's no fun. It's too simple." But they were wrong. Writing your name ought to be easy, but not the way Myra had us do it. When she explained, there was a stir* of excitement in the class. She had us go to the blackboard, five students at a time. "Now write your name," she said, and everyone wrote their name. Easy. "Now write it again, but this time do it while you lift your left foot and move it in a circle." When we tried, no one could do it. We all screamed with laughter and delight*. When it came my turn, I couldn't do it either, but it was fun. Yesterday was fun and so was today, but I still wish I didn't have to go to camp.*

July, 10

Tonight, when Mom and Peter weren't around, I told Dad I didn't like summer camp. I didn't dare come right out and tell him I wanted to quit, so I told him how miserable* I was. Dad looked concerned*. "What's wrong?" he asked. I told him I was really having a hard time. "I don't understand English," I said, "so I can't help making mistakes. I'm always nervous and worried about doing the wrong thing. I really hate not being able to understand what's going on in class. I'm always the one who gets things wrong." Dad nodded sympathetically*. I told him what made things even harder was that all my classmates looked alike to me. I couldn't tell them apart. Dad was surprised. "Really?" he asked and his eyes sparkled* for a second. He thought I was joking. I was afraid he might laugh, but he didn't. "Please, Dad," I pleaded*. "I'm really suffering*. The only kids I recognize are the two who sit on either side of me." Dad was very understanding. He told me he'd take care of it. I've got the best Dad in the whole world. No one understands me like Dad.*

July, 11

Mom is a tree lover. Today she took Peter and me to Sacramento just to see some trees. Dad was busy, so we had to go by bus. Sacramento is the capital of California. There are all kinds of trees planted around the capital building. Each of them has a label* with the name and where it comes from. Ever since Mom heard about these trees, she's been wanting to see them. After breakfast the three of us waited at the bus stop for the Sacramento bus. The ride took over an hour. When we got there, Mom took out a map and studied the street signs. We'd never been to Sacramento before. We felt like explorers* in an unknown* land. Some of the people on the streets looked very strange, too. Luckily, the Capital Building was close by. Mom loved it. We walked slowly around the whole area and Mom looked closely at each tree. "Aren't they beautiful," she would say. Afterwards, we had something to eat in a nearby restaurant and then came home. I don't love trees the way Mom does, but going to a strange town was exciting.*

June
July
August
September

July, 12

Today Dad said we were going to another kind of supermarket. "Aren't they all the same?" Peter asked. "No," Dad said. "This one is different. You can find many things there other stores don't have. Besides, today you two are going to get some practice using American money." As soon as we entered the store, I noticed a special aroma in the air. It smelled quite wonderful. It made me feel good. But the food on the shelves still looked the same. Where was that nice smell coming from? Dad gave each of us $5.00, and told us we each could buy something for ourselves. The $5.00 was all in coins! We had to figure out* the exact price. I wandered up and down the aisles*. At last I discovered where the special aroma was coming from. It was the fresh coffee beans. Mom and Dad are both coffee drinkers. They like strong coffee made directly from coffee beans. I don't mind coffee if it has cream and sugar in it. Mom says I ruin good coffee by polluting it.*

July, 13

I was a little surprised when Mom woke me up to go to camp this morning. I guess Dad hadn't said anything to her yet. Then, shortly after lunch, Dad showed up at our classroom. I was surprised to see him. "At last," I thought, "my days of suffering are over!" I was sure he'd come to take me away. Rusty shook hands with Dad and they talked for several minutes. Then Rusty turned to the class and announced, "O.K., everybody. Diane's father has brought his camera along to take a picture of our group." All the kids buzzed* with pleasure. Some looked back to smile at me. Rusty distributed* large cards to each of us. He assigned* each of us a number and told us to write it on our card. "Make sure you write clearly." he said. Then he turned to me and said, "Diane, you sit in the middle." I sat down and all the girls sat on either side of me. The boys stood in the back row. Dad said, "Now hold your cards under your chins and smile!" Afterwards, Dad thanked us and left. But he didn't take me with him. How come? Did he forget?*

June
July
August
September

July, 14

It's midsummer and the days can be very hot. Sometimes the temperature goes up to 38 degrees. Every day the skies are sunny and clear and I love it. Sunshine always makes me feel happy. When I go swimming, I like the feel of the sun drying the water from my arms and legs. I swim every day after camp, and I'm getting quite dark. Too dark, Mom says. The other day a lady came up to me and said something in a strange language. She saw my black hair and dark skin and thought I was Mexican. She spoke to me in Spanish. Mom thought it was funny. She said, "If someone from Africa starts talking to you, I'm not going to let you swim any more." Mom likes to joke. I said, "If you do that, I'll do my swimming at night." Actually, I like swimming at night. It's a special feeling. On some nights the stars seem caught in the water. I slip in and move among them. Floating, I look up at the heavens and feel like I am one with them, moving through space on my own lonely journey*. Just me and the stars.*

July, 15

Today just as we were getting set to go over to the pool, Dad showed up again. He brought the photos he had taken the other day, one for each of us, plus one for Rusty. That's when I understood the reason for the picture. Class photos are always taken at the end of a semester, not the beginning. It meant Dad was going to let me drop out of the program. Today would be my last day. The photo would be a remembrance*. Rusty had me give everyone a picture. All the kids were delighted. The photos were a surprise, and they didn't need to pay for them. Dad said, "I can't stay. I've got to hurry back to the office." Dad waved as he drove off and all the kids shouted and waved goodbye. I think I understand why he didn't take me. He wanted me to enjoy one final day of swimming. Afterwards, some of the kids came up and told me how much they liked the class picture. "Gee, Diane, your Dad is a good photographer." At least that's what I think they said. I can't be sure. And I'm not even sure who said it.*

June
July
August
September

July, 16

Dear Aunt Sally:

We've been here for almost a month. So many things have happened. When we first arrived in San Francisco, we were living in a hotel. The hotel stood on a hill in the middle of the city and was very beautiful. The streets in San Francisco are very steep. I was surprised. We saw the cable cars* going up and down the hill. We didn't have time to do any sightseeing*. Dad has promised to bring us back some day soon for a real tour. I'm looking forward to it. Now we're settled in this small, quiet town. Dad says this is a 'University town' because of the nice university located here. He said there are very few towns like this left in America. We've rented a nice house with a swimming pool. The house is surrounded by big trees. There is a park nearby. Peter and I are attending summer camp. To tell the truth, it was terrible the first two weeks. I'm still not used to it and hope I can quit. The other children are all nice, except* they only speak English. Mom, Dad, Peter and I are fine. Say "Hi" to everyone for us.

Love,
Diane

July, 17

Tonight when Dad told me, "I've got some news for you." I was so excited. This had to be what I'd been waiting for. And when he said, "In the future you won't have to ever worry again about not being able to recognize your classmates." I clapped my hands with glee. This was really the best kind of news. In my mind's eye I could already see myself lying by the pool for the rest of the summer, improving my swimming, getting darker. For a moment I felt kind of guilty*. What about Rusty? "Did Rusty say anything when you told him I was quitting?" After all, Rusty had been so nice to me. What would he think? "Quitting?" Dad looked surprised. "Who said anything about quitting?" My heart began to sink. "Didn't I tell you I would take care of it?" Dad said. "Well, I have. Here," he said and handed me a piece of paper. It was a list of all the kids in our class, together with their numbers in the photo. "I got this from Rusty. Start studying after dinner," Dad said. "First quiz at 10:00 p.m."*

June July August September

July, 18

After breakfast, we went with Mom to the Farmer's Market. The Farmer's Market is held outside, in one of the parks. They only have it two days a week. On market days, farmers from the surrounding countryside bring their produce here to sell. Mom said all the fruits and vegetables were very good quality*. There were lots of people buying things. Mom bought some vegetables. She said the prices were very reasonable*. There was also a man there selling crystals*. I'd never seen natural crystals before. I thought they were fascinating*. The man told me they were thousands of years old. He said these came from Arkansas. I stood there looking at them, thinking how nice it would be to have one, when Mom walked over. "My goodness," she said. "These are so lovely." She must have seen the longing* in my eyes. She said, "You don't have to say it. I know." Now, my new crystal is sitting next to me on my bed as I write. Whenever I look at it, I feel so happy.*

July, 19

This town is built around a university. Every time we drive somewhere, either on the way out or on the way back, we always pass the university campus. Each time I try to see as far into the campus as I can, but it's hard. It's like being given a present in a box, but you're not allowed to open it just yet, so you try very hard to guess what's inside. I think all kids know this feeling. That's how I feel whenever we pass the university. Today, we passed there again, for what must be the 108th time. I couldn't stand it anymore, and I asked Dad, "Can anyone visit the campus?" Dad said, yes. "Then why don't you take us there? I'd really like to see it." Dad smiled and said, "Just be patient. I'm saving the best for the last. Besides, I'm too busy now. In another week or two, I'll have a day off. I promise we'll go then." Peter grumbled, "What's so special about visiting a university?" Dad smiled and said, "You're going to be surprised, Peter. You'll like it." Dad always tells us to be patient. I hate waiting. Especially for surprises.*

July, 20

Dad told me to think of learning English as a road. To get to your destination, you have to travel it, step by step. There are no shortcuts*. He said for me, the first step would be to learn the names of my classmates. And now, I know every one of them. Today, for the first time in three weeks, I felt confident. But it wasn't easy. Last night Dad tested me again and I still didn't do well. After dinner, Dad said, "No TV," so I went back to my room to stare* at the photo. No use. When I came out an hour later, I still only could name 1/4 of the kids. Dad said, "You're not paying attention. Don't just look at one person's eyes and another person's jaw*. Never mind the clothes they wear. You've got to look at the entire face. It's like learning to read Chinese characters. You don't look at one corner, or one stroke*; you look at the whole thing. If you think of faces as written words, you won't have any trouble." It worked. Now I not only know the name of every kid in the room, I even know their numbers in the photo.*

July, 21

We played a game called Zip/Zap today. It's supposed to be an easy game, but it was hard for me. We all sat in a big circle. Then Rusty explained how the game is played. I could understand nearly everything he said, but I was still nervous. Rusty told us the person who is "it" will say either ZIP or ZAP. If they say "ZIP" and point to you, you have to say the name of the person on your right. If they say "ZAP", you have to say the name of the person on your left. The person who says the wrong name then becomes "it." I wasn't too worried because now I know the names of all the kids. Rusty told me to start off by being "it." "Just say either ZIP or ZAP and point at someone," he said. But when I tried to say ZIP, it didn't come out right. At first the class laughed, but stopped when they saw I was really having trouble. Rusty tried to help, but it was no use. I just couldn't say it right. Tonight I asked Dad, and he told me "Z" is a hard sound for Chinese to pronounce. Dad's ZIPs and ZAPs are perfect.

June July August September

July, 22

Today was swimming day. Now that I know the names of my classmates, it's more and more fun. Last week I had trouble telling one from the other. Not anymore. Today Michelle, Nancy, Colleen, Andrea and I were diving for a quarter. One person would throw the coin in the water and we'd watch closely to see where it landed on the bottom. Then we'd dive in to see who could grab it first. It was so much fun! A silver coin isn't easy to find in the water. At first we used a penny, but Nancy said a penny was too easy to see. She wanted to change to a quarter, so we did. The other girls are bigger than I am. When they dive into the water, they always get to the coin before I do. Once, Michelle had already picked up the coin, but it fell from her hand as she started up. I was right below her and I caught it. Colleen and Andrea tried to grab it from my hand. We all pulled and tugged and burst out of the water laughing. I wish we had swimming everyday. I wonder if the other girls are as tired as I am tonight.*

July, 23

That first morning, when the whole class called out, "Hi, Diane," I felt it was genuine friendliness. All the kids are very nice, even if they seem to avoid me a little bit. I mentioned* this to Mom, and she said, "Well, put yourself in their place. How would you feel if a stranger, who didn't speak Chinese, came to your school in Taipei? Even if you wanted to be friends, you couldn't. They just don't know what to say to you, that's all." That's true, and I agree with what Mom says. But I'm beginning to realize there's someone in the class who is really unfriendly to me. I don't know who it is, but it seems to be one of the boys. Whenever the class plays games, I sometimes get mixed up and make a mistake. The teachers are patient, and so are the other classmates. But I've noticed when that happens, there is one person who mumbles* something unfriendly. It's always the same voice. Today Rusty told him to stop. I didn't dare look around to see who it was. I don't really want to know.*

June
July
August
September

July, 24

Simon is one face I never had trouble recognizing. Even in the early days of camp, before I got to know the names of everyone, I knew who Simon was. He's bigger than the rest of the kids. He's also a bully. I don't know how the other kids feel, but I don't like him. Whenever we have an art project, Myra almost always praises Simon's work. Sometimes she'll even hold it up in front of the class for all of us to admire*. Today Myra showed us some pictures of wild animals. She told us to choose one to draw. I chose a leopard*. Afterwards, Myra said it was the best in the class. I don't know if Myra really meant it, or was just trying to encourage me. Anyway, it was a good feeling. She told me to stand up in front and show the class. The other kids all looked respectful*. Some of them even seemed to genuinely admire my leopard. Not Simon. He just sat there and looked sullen*. I could see anger in his eyes. All because of a picture? It's hard to believe. I'd better stay clear of* him.*

July, 25

This morning the shipping company phoned. Our furniture has arrived from Taiwan. It will be delivered to our house on Monday. We're all very excited. Mom phoned Dad at the office to tell him the news. Dad said he's going to take the day off so we can put the house in order right away. He doesn't want to wait until the weekend. I asked Dad if Peter and I could stay home on Monday, too, but he refused. "There'll be plenty of time when you come home from camp," he said. At dinner tonight we talked about what things would go in what rooms. Actually, we talked about this when we first moved in, but that was when our house was new and strange. Now that our things have actually arrived, we're planning all over again. It's fun to plan. Now I'm sitting on my bed and trying to imagine how to arrange my own room. It's strange, but I'm not sure which things Mom packed for me. Oh well, it doesn't matter. I feel like something special is going to happen. I can hardly wait.*

June July August September

July, 26

This afternoon Dad was browsing through downtown bookstores. Peter and I felt bored. We asked Dad if we could walk over to the train station. He said, "Go ahead, but be back in half an hour." When we first came to town, we stayed in a hotel right behind the train station. We never had a chance to go there. Peter said, "Let's take a look. It'll be fun to see what kind of people take the train." So off we went. The station is very small. There weren't many people waiting, but they all looked very happy. I guess they were thinking about their coming journey. In the distance we heard a horn*. Peter and I hurried out to look. A beautiful shining engine slowly pulled into the station. Behind it was a long line of passenger cars. "Wow! It looks so new," Peter exclaimed*. "Doesn't it look nice." When everyone got on board, the train started to pull away*. The conductor* waved to us and we waved back. The train looked so sleek* and powerful. I wish I could get on that train, too.*

July, 27

When I got home from camp, a large truck was parked in front of our house. Our Taiwan furniture had arrived! The truck driver and his helper unloaded everything and moved them into the house for us. They asked what rooms we wanted them in, but we told them to just put everything in the living room. We opened the crates eagerly. It was like meeting old familiar friends again. All my personal treasures were there. I gathered them up and put them in my bedroom, along with my crystal and other things. Mom had packed her favorite chair and blackwood desk. Mom loves wood and she had fallen in love with these the first time she set eyes on them in an antique* shop. Dad had shipped his bookshelves and all his books. "Books make a home" is one of his favorite sayings. Mom looked at all these things and said, "Well, it's going to be hard work putting all these where they belong." But she said it with a smile and we all knew she was happy. It's been a busy, happy day.*

July, 28

Well, I think I discovered today who doesn't like me. When I came to class this morning, Simon was standing outside the door. If I'd seen him earlier, I would have avoided him, but it was too late. As I walked up to the door, he stared at me with his mean* little eyes. I gave him my usual smile, but he just snorted* and turned away. I'm certain he's the one who's been making unfriendly remarks* every time I make a mistake. Simon was standing with some older boys from another group. They all laughed loudly when they saw him ignore* my greeting. I don't think he's upset* just because Myra praised my drawing. No, I think he probably didn't like me from the very beginning. Myra's praise only made it worse*. I'd never wanted to know which classmate disliked* me. I thought that maybe after I learned a little English, whoever it was would gradually change their mind. Well, it's too late now. If he tries to say anything to me, I'll just smile and pretend I don't understand.

July, 29

Something really strange happened today. One moment I was standing at the edge of the pool talking to Sandra and Claire. The next moment I was hurtling through the air. Sky and pool turned upside down. I hit the water, hard. I came up, choking* and sputtering* and heard Sandra say angrily, "You pushed her on purpose, Simon. I saw you!" An innocent* looking Simon replied, "Not me. She must have slipped*." I'd had enough of Simon. "No I didn't," I burst out. My English was suddenly like a river breaking through* its banks. "You did it on purpose. You're always making trouble. Everybody knows it." I surprised myself. I didn't have to think what to say. The words came by themselves, just like Dad said they someday would. Everyone looked at me, startled*. "And you'd better not try that again or you'll be sorry," I warned him. "Oh, yeah?" Simon said defiantly*, but then Rusty walked up. "I saw the whole thing, Simon," he said. "Get out of the pool. No more swimming for you for two weeks."*

June July August September

July, 30

This morning Myra told us we were going to create "Fantastic Creatures." She had prepared about 30 different pictures of wild animals, birds and even some cartoon animals from Disney movies. "O.K., kids. Each one of you is going to create your own fantastic animal. I want you to use your own imagination. Don't copy your neighbor." Some of the kids looked helpless. They didn't know what to do. Not me. I looked across the room at Simon. He was wearing black pants and a white shirt with pink stripes*. I put my head down and started to work. Simon has the habit of always looking over his shoulder. I first drew a large wolf's head looking slyly* over his shoulder, the way Simon always does. Then I gave it a boy's body and dressed him in the same black pants and shirt Simon was wearing. Finally, I drew a long rat's tail sticking out* behind. Afterwards, when we showed our picture, the class screamed with delight. They knew exactly who it was.*

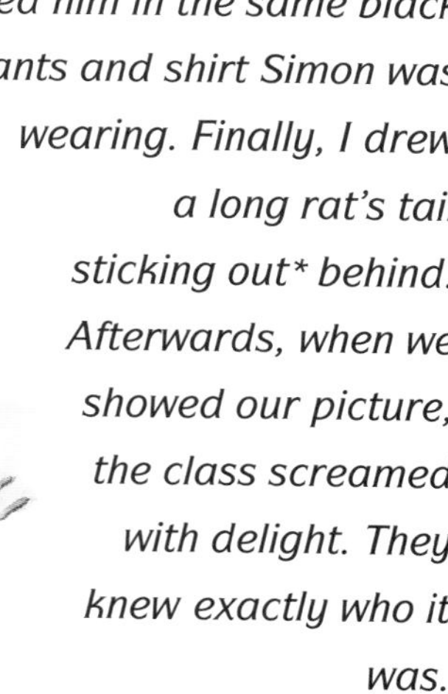

July, 31

Today Claire and Melanie walked home with me. They live in the same direction as I do. In the past they've never asked me to walk with them. To tell the truth, I wouldn't have wanted to. I could hardly speak English. It would have been awkward, both for them and for me. So they walked on one side of the street, and I walked on the other. If our eyes met, we would smile and say "Hi," but most of the time they pretended not to notice me. That was O.K. with me. After all, what could we talk about? We had nothing in common. But today, everything changed. It seems as if every kid in class came over to talk with me. Well, not all of them. Not Simon, of course. He doesn't even look in my direction. With yesterday's "Fantastic Creature" exercise, the other kids discovered I have a sense* of fun and they love it. Dad says a sense of fun is a kind of a language. All kids understand it, no matter what country they come from. I'd never thought of it that way.*

June

July

August

September

August, 1

There's a donut shop in the university mall. Every time we go to the market in the mall, there are always many people sitting inside, drinking coffee or tea and having a donut. But we've never gone in. Today, after shopping, Dad and Mom decided we should try their donuts. I was surprised to see that the owner is Chinese. Each of us ordered a donut. Mom and Dad also ordered coffee. When I bit into my donut, I swear* it was the most delicious donut I had ever tasted! The owner came over to serve the coffee. He asked us where we were from. Dad told him we were from Taiwan. He gave us a warm smile and said in Mandarin, "I'm from Taiwan, too." He sat down and chatted* with us for a few minutes. "My son works at the university," he said. "I opened this donut shop to pass the time." When we were ready to leave, he insisted* that it was on the house*. Afterwards, Dad remarked about how nice the owner had been, but all I could think about was how soon can I come here again for more donuts.*

August, 2

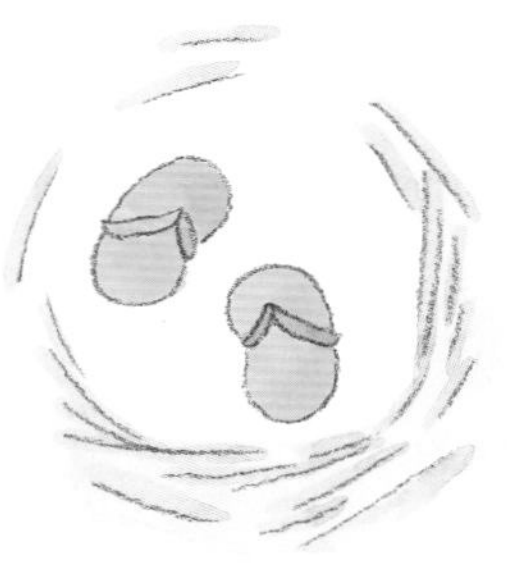

I've never paid attention to the two-story house behind us. It's hidden behind a big tree and is almost invisible. Today, while I was sitting by our pool, daydreaming, a bird flew down from the big tree. I was curious and watched to see what it was doing. It jumped about on our lawn for a while, happily hunting for food. The hunting looked pretty good. Then the thought struck me. "My goodness! He's eating worms*!" Ugh! How was I going to get back to the house? I hadn't brought my slippers with me. The thought of walking barefoot across our lawn and squashing* millions of worms under my bare feet was just too horrible. Just as I was wondering what to do, the bird flew back up to the tree again. I tried to see it, but he was gone. He had disappeared among the leaves. Through the leaves I saw a flash of movement. I looked again, more closely. That's when I noticed the window. Had someone been watching me, or if not me, watching our pool?*

"Who would that be?" I wondered.

June July August September

August, 3

Dear Diane:

Thank you for your letter. I'm sorry to hear you had a terrible time at first. Things are bound to get better. I'm sure the worst time is already behind you. By the time you read this letter, I'll bet you're already starting to have fun. San Francisco must be a wonderful city. I've never been there. Lucky Diane. How I wish I were you! I wonder if I'll ever have time to travel again. Right now I have a dream. If things work out*, maybe your uncle and I can come to visit you next year. See? Even old people have their little dreams. Coming to see all of you is my dream. I envy you living in a big house with trees and, yes, even your own swimming pool! It sounds too good to be true. Oh yes, your friend Julie called a few days ago. She asked for your address. She said she will pass it on* to your friends. Don't be surprised if you start getting a lot of letters. Everyone here wants to know more about your new life. Please write us often.*

Love,

Aunt Sally

August, 4

Today I told Peter about seeing something in the house behind us. "You think somebody was watching you?" Peter asked. "Come to think of it, I've never seen anybody around there," he said. Peter was silent for a moment, thinking. "Let's go over and check it out." "You mean climb over the back fence?" I asked. "No, stupid. That's too obvious*. We'll just walk over to that street and look from the outside." As we walked along, Peter counted the number of houses to the end of the block. Seven. Then we turned the corner and started up the street behind us. The seventh house was a white two-story building. There was a big "FOR SALE" sign in the front yard. I recognized the word "SALE" because Mom showed me once when we were shopping. The house had no feeling of life about it. There was no sign of movement in the windows. I don't know why, but it looked threatening*. Peter said, "Let's get out of here," and we hurried quickly back to the safety of our own street.

June
July
August
September

August, 5

Swimming was extra nice today because I didn't have to worry about Simon. He still has to wait another week before Rusty will let him swim again. I really love swimming. Mom says I must have been a fish in a past life. That made me think. If everyone has a past life, I wonder what Simon was in his past life. Something pretty terrible, for sure. Maybe a snake. Not just any snake, but a poisonous snake. Or maybe a monkey? I saw a film on TV last week about monkeys in India. It seemed to me they were always jumping around, pushing one another. The way they acted reminded me of Simon. I suppose it's not nice to think like this. It's an insult* to snakes and monkeys. I tried to think of Simon as some other kind of animal, but none of them seemed right. Certainly not a lion. A lion is fierce* and brave. Well, it doesn't matter. He lives here in the same town, and we're in the same summer camp. Simon's a pest*, but even he can't spoil* swimming for me.*

August, 6

This morning at breakfast Dad said, "School will be starting soon. It's time for you kids to have bikes." Peter and I were surprised. Our school will be within walking distance. We never expected Dad would let us have bikes. During camp today, I kept thinking about having my own bicycle. I didn't concentrate* as I should and made more mistakes than usual. As a result I wound up* being "it" most of the time. But I didn't mind. The only trouble is, I don't know how to ride a bike. Peter is better than me, but not much. Bike riding in Taipei is too dangerous. We never had a chance to learn. When we first moved here we were surprised to see so many people riding bikes. Not just children, but university students and many adults as well. This town is designed for bike riding. There are special bike lanes* on all the busier streets. The reasons are obvious. Bike riding helps keep the air clean and it's good for the health. Everyone seems to own one. Now I was about to become one of them.*

June
July
August
September

August, 7

After dinner, Dad suggested we go out for a walk. We all cheered. After sunset, cool air moves into the valley from San Francisco Bay. The nights are cool and comfortable. There was no one else on the street. As we walked through the moonlight, Mom took a deep breath. "Isn't this wonderful," she said, "We could never enjoy this kind of air in Taipei!" Mom was right. The air here seems different. For one thing, there is a fragrance at night. I don't know what kind of plant it comes from, but I always notice it when we take our evening walks. In the park, the moon seemed to be hanging* low on a tree. I felt that if one climbed that tree, they could reach out and take the moon down from the sky. "The moon here is so big and round," I said. Mom said, "Haven't you heard? The foreign moon is rounder." We all laughed. This is a common joke in Taiwan. But it's true. The moon here is larger. Peter was the only one who didn't seem to enjoy the moon. "It's too bright," he said. "It pushes all the stars away. They've been squeezed* to the edges of the sky." Mom liked that idea. "That's pretty imaginative*, Peter." She said. Peter's words made me think. Maybe everyone in the world is either a moon person or a star person. Peter's obviously a star guy. Me, I like moons.*

August, 8

This morning, Dad finally took us on a tour of the university campus. He had been promising to do this ever since we came here, but never had time. This is the school Dad attended when he came to America to study. He had often told us how happy he'd been here and how beautiful the campus was. I never imagined it would be so lovely. Dad took us all over the campus, pointing out the various buildings. Later we went over to the Student Center for lunch. Peter and I had pizza. After lunch, we went outside and sat at a table in the shade* of nearby trees. Surrounded by the campus he loved, Dad sat back and began to talk. He wanted us to understand how it felt for him, a country boy, to come all the way from Taiwan to this quiet university town, 20 years ago. He wanted us to know what the experience had meant to him. He talked until the shadows grew longer and there were very few people about. I sat there, listening carefully. I didn't want to ever forget what he was saying.*

August, 9

Yesterday this is what Dad said, "When I was young I was a good student. I don't mean to say I was smart or that I even liked school. In fact I didn't. But I knew what had to be done, and did it. My grades were always good, but frankly, I found many of the subjects boring because the teachers didn't present* them well. Then when I came here, things were different. The first day I stepped on the campus, I could feel it. I spent three years here and loved every minute of it. Many of my professors* were thoughtful and patient. They didn't just teach. They guided me. They treated me like an adult, a professional equal*. On occasion they invited me to their house and I got to know their wives and families. I've kept in touch with many of my classmates over the years and now have dozens of friends all over the world. Not everyone felt the same way. I've talked to other students, both American and foreign, who didn't like it here. Some of them transferred to other schools. But for me, at that stage in my life, it was the perfect place."*

August, 10

Dear Aunt Sally,

Thank you for your letter. You are right. I'm starting to have fun. I made some friends in summer camp. I have learned how to speak a little English. Remember when we went to the beach last summer at Fulung? I didn't know how to swim then. Here in summer camp, our class has swimming every Wednesday afternoon. But they don't teach you how to swim. All the kids already know how. So we just play around and have fun. At first, I really felt the pressure*. The first day we had swimming class, I didn't bring a swimsuit because I didn't understand what my teacher said. It was really embarrassing. I had to sit out while the others played. I made up my mind right then to learn how to swim. Everyday after camp I went home and practiced and practiced. Now I can swim pretty good and I'm not afraid of the water anymore. In fact, I love it. Next time we meet, we can have a race. Please tell everyone not to worry. We are getting used to American life.

Love,

Diane

June

July

August

September

August, 11

After I get home from camp, I usually go right outside to the pool. Sometimes I swim for a while, sometimes I just sit there and daydream. But these last few days I haven't gone out to the pool at all. Mom thought I was sick and insisted on taking my temperature. Of course it was normal. How could I tell her I was afraid of that mysterious window out in back? Let's face it. I'm afraid of what might be in that empty house. In other words, I'm afraid of ghosts. Ever since Peter and I discovered the house behind us was empty, I haven't felt comfortable in our yard. From that day on, I imagined terrible things taking place in that house. Did someone die there? If the person who was looking through that window was a child, was he looking for a playmate? And did he ever come out at night, and look into our windows? Once I began to think about these things, terrible images* popped up* into my mind. I think I'd better turn off the light and go to sleep. No. I'll leave the light on.*

August, 12

Rusty reminded us today there are only three weeks remaining of camp. That means only three more swimming classes. He said all the summer groups will get together for a final swimming competition* on the 27th of August. Even though our town is small, the Community Center has five separate* summer camps. Each camp is located in a different part of town. In our final swimming class, each group will hold races* to select the best swimmers. Everyone will participate*. The best swimmers will then compete* for the summer camp championship* on the 27th. Just thinking about it makes me nervous. After all, I just learned to swim this summer. I'm improving, but the thought of a race scares me. I don't want to wind up in last place. I told Rusty I didn't want to race, but he just laughed and said, "Don't worry about it. It'll be fun." Tonight I asked Dad if I could stay home that day, but Dad said, "Don't worry. It'll be fun." I'd expect Dad to say that sort of thing. I'd hoped for more sympathy* from Rusty.*

August, 13

Mom told us Uncle Ted will be coming to stay with us this Sunday. Uncle Ted is an old friend of Dad's. They've known each other since junior high school. After military service, they both came to the university here for graduate study. Dad studied engineering and Uncle Ted studied dentistry* at the medical school. After graduation, Uncle Ted stayed on in America and now has his own dental clinic* in San Francisco. His wife and son will be coming along with him. Dad and Uncle Ted haven't seen each other for several years. When we were in San Francisco in June, Dad was too busy to get together with him. Tonight at dinner Dad told us about some of the things he and Uncle Ted used to do when they were teenagers. Some of them sound really crazy. Dad always smiles when he tells these stories. I wonder if someday I'll ever feel the same way when I look back on my days in summer camp? I don't think so. After all, there was no Simon around when Dad and Ted were kids.*

August, 14

I finally got up courage to go out to the pool today. At first, I just put my face against the big glass window facing the pool, and looked out. The sky outside was so clear. There wasn't a cloud to be seen. The trees glittered in the sunlight, their leaves dancing in the light breeze*. I could almost hear their rustling* voice inside the house. The pool was blue, too. It was like a mirror reflecting* the sky. The lawn looked soft, like a lush* carpet, inviting me to come out and step on it. I looked closely towards the hidden window. It looked perfectly normal. The curtains were drawn. "Maybe I was over-reacting that day," I told myself. "Maybe there was no movement behind that window at all." I waited another two minutes. The temptation out there was just too great. I opened the glass door. "At least I'm not going to squash those worms with my bare feet," I thought. I stepped into my slippers, and ran. I rushed over the green carpet, ignoring the screams of dying worms, and jumped into the pool. It was wonderful.*

August, 15

Well, window or no window, I've got to work hard on my swimming. Right now I'm more afraid of finishing last than of whatever might be watching me from that window. Today I swam widths, instead of lengths. That way I didn't have to look up and wonder about what might be standing in that window. Tonight at dinner, Mom told Peter and me we had to straighten up our rooms tomorrow. "I want the house to be neat and clean when Uncle Ted gets here," she said. She told us we couldn't go out to play until our rooms were cleaned. It didn't matter to me. I always keep my things in order. But Peter is different. He's kind of sloppy*. He always tosses* his things on the floor or on the chair when he's finished. To tell the truth, his room is a mess. He can never find anything when he wants it. He always has to ask Mom to help him. "Aw, Mom," he said. "Can't I just close the door when they get here? That way no one can see if my room's messy or not." Peter has some strange ideas about housekeeping.*

August, 16

Uncle Ted, his wife, Aunt Ruby, and their son Arthur, arrived just in time for lunch today. While the adults talked happily about old times, I eyed Arthur, sitting across from us at the table. He's a year older than Peter. Uncle Ted speaks English very fluently*, but I noticed that even after all these years, he still has trouble pronouncing some words. I noticed it because I had the same problem at the beginning of summer. Anyway, no one spoke much English today. Except for Arthur, that is. If you speak to Arthur in Chinese, he answers in English. After lunch, while the adults talked, Peter and I took Arthur to the park. He insisted on talking English the whole time. Perhaps he feels because we've only been here since summer, our English can't be very good and he wants to show off*. It could also be that his Chinese isn't so good. I don't know. Now I'm getting ready to go to sleep and Dad and Uncle Ted are still talking.*

June July August September

August, 17

This morning I heard Uncle Ted telling Dad about an interesting theory he had read a short while back. A famous Swiss psychiatrist*, Dr. Jung, claims* that people acquire* the soul* of the land where they grow up, no matter what race* they might be. I could tell Uncle Ted was thinking about Arthur. This afternoon Peter and I showed Arthur around our neighborhood. He didn't seem too interested. All the time he kept talking about how wonderful San Francisco is. While he was talking, I watched him closely. If Dr. Jung's theory was correct, Arthur might reveal* his Indian soul, and start whooping* like Indians do in the movies. But nothing happened. I was kind of disappointed. As they prepared to leave, Aunt Ruby said, "Don't wait too long to come and see us." Then they waved and were gone. As their car disappeared down the street, Peter asked, "When are we going to San Francisco, Dad?" It looks like Arthur's stories of life in the big city have got him fired up*.*

August, 18

Dear Diane,

I phoned your aunt and she gave me your address. Do you like your new life? I certainly envy you being able to live in California. I asked my mom if I could go to America to study, like you. Well, you can guess the answer was "No!" But she said when I grow up, maybe I can go abroad to study. Honestly, Diane, I don't think I can wait that long! It takes forever to grow up, don't you think so? Especially when the time passes so slowly, like during school. It seems time only passes quickly during summer and vacation. How about America? Does American time pass any faster? As your best friend, you simply must tell me everything you've been doing. Mom signed me up to study English this summer. At first I didn't want to go. But now that you're in America, it gives me some kind of link with English. I'm studying hard, but good heavens, English is so difficult. What about you? Do you speak English now? Write me! Don't wait. Do it tonight!

Your friend,

Julie

June July August September

August, 19

Today, Rusty taught us how to do a racing dive. "Be sure you dive shallow," he warned. "If you dive too deep, you'll be left behind." Dive? I don't know how to dive. I can only jump in the water, feet first. Rusty watched while each of us tried a racing dive. When it was my turn, I landed with a loud splat*. But it wasn't a racing dive. I had landed flat on my stomach. It was what the kids call a "belly* flop*," and it hurt. Usually people laugh when someone does a belly flop, but not today. Everyone was serious. Rusty came over to help me. "Just lean* forward, Diane, and keep looking at your feet. The dive will take care of itself." I wasn't so sure, but I did as he said, and it worked! Just like Rusty said it would. I made a perfect dive. The only trouble is, I went right to the bottom of the pool. "Diane," Rusty said, "if you dive that deep in a race, the race will be finished by the time you come back up." We practiced racing dives for another thirty minutes. Only seven days to go. I'm really nervous.

August, 20

When summer camp first started, Myra often praised Simon for his artwork. All the kids considered him a pretty good artist. I guess he's O.K., but now Myra has complimented* my work two times and it obviously bothers him. Sandra says he's making trouble for me because he's jealous. Claire says that's why he pushed me in the pool last week. I don't think it had anything to do with art. I think Simon is just a troublemaker, a naturally mean kid. Today we had another art project. Simon tried to draw a picture of me that would make me look bad. When he held it up for everyone to see, Myra said, "You've got to be more original*, Simon. That's the same thing Diane did last week, only she did it better." All the kids laughed, but not at the picture. They were laughing at Simon. Simon and I seem to be at war. And so far, he's losing.

August, 21

This afternoon I went with Mom to the shopping mall. I was hoping we could go to the donut shop again, but Mom was in a hurry. As we walked in, some girls from camp were riding by on their bikes. I looked longingly at their bikes. I wish I had one. If I had a bike, then I could ride around like the other girls. One of them saw me, and called out, "Diane!" It was Candy. The other three girls were Susan, Beatrice and Louise. They all pulled up and said hello. Mom said, "You stay and talk with your friends. I'll be right back." We talked about the coming swim meet*. We wondered who the best swimmers would be. Beatrice said there was a girl named Rachel from one of the other camps. She said Rachel was a really good swimmer. We stood there talking and laughing until Mom came back. Afterwards, when we were in the car, Mom said, "You know, I was watching you just now. You surprised me. You can really speak English now." It was my turn to be surprised. Mom's words made me realize I hadn't worried about English for a long time.

August, 22

Dear Julie,

I'm so happy to hear from you. Yes, I like my new life here. But I have to admit, at first it wasn't so easy for me. I had to go to summer camp without being able to speak a single word of English! Anyway, I'm getting used to it by now. And, yes, I'm even speaking English. My mom told me yesterday that I'm pretty good. In your letter you said you wanted to know everything that has happened. Oh, Julie, there are so many things, I don't know where to start! I'd better first try and tell you a little bit about this place. The town where we live is a university town. Normally there are thousands of students going to school here, but because it's summer vacation, there aren't many people around. The neighborhood where we live is quiet and beautiful. We like to go out in the evening and take a walk. It is very strange that we hardly ever see other people out walking. Dad said Americans love their cars. They can't live without them. That seems to be true. Well, time to turn my light out. I'll write more next time.*

Your friend,

Diane

June July August September

August, 23

I reminded Dad today about getting us bicycles. I've been thinking about having a bike ever since he first mentioned it. Dad said he hadn't forgotten. "As a matter of fact," he said, "I was planning to go bike hunting today." I thought we would go to the bicycle store at the mall, but Dad had a different idea. He took us to a shop near the university. "Great, they're still here," Dad said in excitement. It was a store that sold only second-hand bicycles. Dad said that when he came here as a student, this is where he bought his bike. We went in and looked around. Dad picked out two bikes. One for each of us kids. Then he chose two more: one for Mom and one for himself. All four bikes looked like they needed painting. Dad said, "As long as they work, an old one is just as good as a new one." That's Dad. Maybe this is why he likes to go to browse in second-hand bookstores. He paid up and we put the bikes on the car. "We'll give them some new paint," Dad said. I can hardly wait to start practicing.*

August, 24

"What color do you like?" Dad asked when we were in the hardware* store. Dad couldn't make up his mind. America's hardware stores are really different from those in Taiwan. They are spacious* and everything is neatly arranged on the shelves. Everything you could possibly need for household maintenance* can be found there. From big machinery like lawn mowers* to small items like nails, it's all there. "I'd like my bike to be blue," Peter said. "Oh, Peter," I wailed, "That's the color I want." "Pick another," Peter told me. "Well, we can always have two blue bikes." Dad said to me, "I don't know." I said. "Let me look around some more." I walked along the aisle where the paints were located. Brown, Blue, Green, ...Pink, Red, ...My gosh, I really didn't know which to choose. "Hurry up, Diane. Make up your mind!" Peter was getting impatient*. Boy, making a decision under that kind of pressure is really tough. "Indigo*!" I finally decided. It's a beautiful blue color. I hope Dad will do a good job on my bike.

June
July
August
September

August, 25

Myra showed us how to make our own kites today. Everybody was excited. I put each piece together very carefully. But some of the girls really had trouble. They couldn't get it right. When all the kites were finished, we went outside to fly them. I ran and ran to make mine fly, and finally it lifted upward. It soared high against the blue sky. Soon, everybody's kite was flying. It looked like the sky was full of strange birds, swooping* and turning. When I was flying the kite, I thought of my grandpa. He made a kite for me once. We cut out every piece of paper and glued them together. Grandpa even found some small bamboo sticks for the kite frame*. He held the bamboo sticks over a small fire so they would bend* the way he wanted. It was a big and colorful kite. When we finished, we went out to the school yard to fly it. It flew up high, just like the one I made today. Suddenly, under the bright blue sky, I thought of Grandpa. I wish I could show my kite to him and invite him to fly it with me.*

August, 26

Today we had races to see who from our class would swim in tomorrow's Summer Camp Championships. The boys raced first while we girls watched. Watching them, I was very nervous. Then it was our turn. Rusty said, "Swimmers, take your mark," and we stepped up, ready to dive. The whistle* blew, and I stretched out as far as I could. When I hit the water, I swam as hard as I could to keep up with the others. As soon as I touched the other end, I raised my head and looked around. Claire came in just behind me. Hooray*! I wasn't the last one. But, what's this? Emma, Sandra, Ruby and Joan all came in behind Claire. Oh, no! This wasn't supposed to happen. I had come in 2nd place, behind Lori. Lori and I will represent our class in the championships. I really regret practicing so hard! Now it's 2:00 a.m. and I still can't sleep. I'm so tired, but I can't stop thinking about tomorrow. I wish we had never come to California. I wish I was back in Taiwan.*

September
August
July
June

August, 27

Had trouble getting up this morning. But I felt O.K. by race time. At the starting whistle, I dove into the water and struggled with all my might* to come up ahead of the other kids. Every time I put my face down, I could glimpse Rachel's arms stroking the water to my right. She was a little ahead of me. I put my head down and drove my arms into the water. Faster, faster, faster. My shoulders were aching and my lungs* were on fire. Kick, kick, reach out, grab more water, pull. Strain* with all my might. I couldn't hear anything, just those strange hollow* sounds when one's head is under water. Where was the wall? Suddenly my hand touched the side. It was over. I raised my head to look, as Rachel splashed up to the finish. She looked up, pale and gasping*. I had won! I had beaten her by about one foot! All the kids were screaming and shouting. Hands reached down to pull me up. I was too tired to climb out of the water. Then I saw Dad. He was jumping and cheering. He had taken the day off to come and see me race. And he'd never said a word.*

August, 28

So much happened today. I want to write it all down. Today was the last day of camp. There was a big barbecue and everyone came; not just us kids, but all their brothers and sisters, and of course the parents. Later, as the first evening star began to twinkle overhead, the director of the summer program rose to speak. It was the same nice lady who had taken Peter and me to our rooms the first day. "At the end of every summer camp," she said, "we always present awards* to those children whom our teachers feel have gotten the most from their summer camp experience." There was a ripple* of excitement among the children as she began to read out the names. I wasn't too interested. I wondered where Claire was. Just as I was looking around for her, I heard my name called. For a second, I was scared. Had I done something wrong? But everyone was looking at me and smiling. Friendly hands pushed me through the crowd and up to the director. The director said, "Congratulations, Diane," and handed me a small plaque* with some words written on it. I didn't know what to say. Everyone laughed, but their laughter was warm and kind.*

June July August September

August, 28

[same day]

Claire came running up and hugged me. "Oh, Diane," she said. "Isn't it wonderful?" I still wasn't sure what the plaque was for. "What does it say, Claire?" I asked. Claire looked at the plaque and read, "Best Swimmer in 8–9 year-old Category!" Best swimmer? Me? I couldn't believe it. Then suddenly Rusty was standing next to us. He bent* down and asked, "Hey, is this the same little girl who forgot her bathing suit the first day?" I felt very shy. I told him I couldn't have done it without him, and I meant it. I couldn't have. "No, you deserved* it," he said. "You worked hard. You really improved. I'm proud of you, Diane." Then, as he turned to go, he added with a smile, "It's too bad they don't have an award for most improvement in English. You'd have won that, too." Then he was gone. Watching him go, I had a funny feeling. I realized that summer was really over. Now it's quite late. I've been writing so much my hand is sore. My plaque is on the dresser, right next to my crystal. I can't stop looking at it. Oh, Rusty, you did this for me. Imagine! Me, a swimmer! I love California. I never want to leave.*

August, 29

Last night even though I was tired, it took me a long time to get to sleep. I was too happy, too excited. This morning, when Mom called me, I had a hard time getting out of bed. Mom wanted to go shopping today. "School starts next week and there are still some things we need to buy for you and Peter." There were signs hanging all over the department store. Mom read them for me, "Back to School." I'd been so busy with swimming I'd never noticed them. But Mom had. She's been getting us ready for school for several days. Mom bought backpacks for us to carry our books in. It seems like everyone has a backpack in this town, especially the university students. I'd been wanting one for a long time. Afterwards I met Sherry and Maureen at the ice cream store. There were some new faces at the mall. Kids that have been away for the summer are now starting to come back. Sherry and Maureen knew most of them, but there were a few they'd never seen before. These must be new kids moving in from out of town, just like me, not so long ago. Only a few short days of vacation left.

June
July
August
September

August, 30

Summer camp has only been over for 2 days and already I miss it. I never thought I would. It's hard to believe. I was so miserable at first that I even asked Dad to let me quit. That seems so long ago. The last week I never wanted it to end. I can't believe 6 weeks have passed. I wonder how I'll feel 6 weeks from now. Right now I feel sad. Myra's going away. Rusty's going back to his adult world. I'll never see either of them again. School next week. New faces. When I think about it I worry. Dad says not to, but I do. He says school is going to be just an extension of summer camp. "You already know lots of the kids," he said, "I know you won't have any trouble." I'd like to believe him, but I'm not so sure. Somehow, I can't help but feel that starting next week, my whole life is going to change. Change is easy for a grown-up, like Dad. But I don't feel so grown-up right now. In fact, I feel scared, just like when summer camp started. And tonight I'm really, really tired. When school starts, I wonder what my life will be like.*

August, 31

Dad phoned this afternoon, which isn't unusual, but this time mother looked upset after she hung up. "What's wrong, Mom?" I asked, and she replied, "I'm not sure." But I wouldn't be put off*, and asked, "Then why do you look so worried?" Mom said, "Dad's company just informed him that we won't be staying on, after all. The Taipei office needs him. We'll have to go back."*

My first reaction was a thrill of relief. I was going to be spared*. I'd been dreading* going to school. I wouldn't ever have to worry about Simon again. Looking back, Summer camp had been relatively easy, especially after the first week or so. But school would be a different matter. Bigger classes, many strange faces. Not only that, but my reading skills weren't very good. Did I say, "Weren't very good?" They were terrible. Zero. It would be like starting all over. Like a space ship landing on a strange planet. Now, I wouldn't have to worry any more.*

Mom was right. Maybe I was too young, but it still didn't seem so terrible to me. But when Dad came home tonight, I began to think differently.

June July August September

September, 1

Peter had been in the park playing football with his friends. He came home just as it was getting dark. When Mom told him the news that night, he looked glum. I knew how badly he wanted to play football this fall. This meant the end of his dreams. But he didn't say anything. I can see Peter's more practical than I am. When Dad came home, the first thing Peter said was, "Dad, what are we going to do about all our things? Gee, if we'd known at the start we were only going to stay a short time, we could have saved all the trouble and money of shipping our things over here. Didn't your company think of that?" Looking more tired than usual, Dad said, "The trouble will be ours. The expense* will be the company's. Because they're sending us back, they pay for everything."*

Alarmed, Peter asked, "Gee, Dad, you haven't been fired, have you?" "No," Dad replied, "Actually, I've been promoted." Promoted! That sounded great to me. I felt like I'd been released from a prison sentence. I couldn't understand why he and Mom looked so distracted*. I said, "Well, what's so bad about that?" Mom said, "You're young and don't have to worry about such things, but moving so soon again is going to mean lots of inconvenience*." My goodness, we've barely gotten used to this place, and now we're going to leave.*

September, 2

This morning when I woke up my excitement had faded. Slowly I'd begun to realize that I'd come to like our small town. In fact, I not only liked it, I loved it. I loved the weather, the safe streets, and the many things there were for kids to do. Little by little, I realized I wasn't so sure I wanted to leave.*

Saying goodbye was going to be hard. When we left Taiwan, saying goodbye to friends and family had been easy. We were only going away for a year, maybe two. We knew we'd be seeing one another someday. But saying goodbye to my friends from summer camp was going to be different. I'd probably never see them again. Just thinking about it made me sad.

Anyhow, one by one, I started telling them I wouldn't be with them when school opened. "Are you going to go to a private school, Diane?" They asked. "No," I said. "My Dad's been transferred back to Taipei." Taiwan sounded so far away to them. They couldn't imagine anyone going to a place so different. Someone else asked, "Can't your father go back by himself? That way you and Peter and your Mom could stay on here until next summer." I had to admit, that was a nice thought, but I'm sure my parents would never go for it.*

June July August September

September, 3

School has already started, so my friends and I are no longer together all day long. Not like we were during the summer. I feel lonely. Peter doesn't say anything, but I can tell he'd rather stay here, in California. He'd probably hoped he could finish high school here. When you think about it, every one has to go their separate way sometime in life. But here in our town that generally doesn't happen until after high school graduation. Then most of the kids scatter* to different colleges, or go to work. But high school graduation was so far in the future we never even thought about it. I suppose kids everywhere are the same, but for us, our lives were right now, this very minute. They didn't like losing a friend, either. When I saw how much they cared for me, I felt even worse. At that moment I wanted to stay and go to school with them more than anything in the world. I could even put up with Simon. Anything. Just so I could stay. I'd really changed these last couple of days. Anyway, Simon and I probably never have been in the same class. It would have been easy to avoid him.

September, 4

One evening, after dinner, I rode my bike through the nearby streets. A couple of more days, and we'll be leaving. The evenings are already chilly and I had to wear a sweater. I wanted to take one last look at my neighborhood. I wanted to make sure I'd never forget it. I wanted to say goodbye to familiar streets and friendly homes. Lights were coming on as the dusk deepened. I imagined what they were doing at that moment. The elderly couple, whose children lived in another town, would be sitting down to dinner. I stopped across the street from Claire's house. Then, one by one, I rode past where all my neighborhood friends lived. I paused across the street from each of their homes. I didn't ring the doorbell, and didn't call them. I just looked and remembered. I even rode through the park, and took a last look at the swimming pool, now locked and silent. It already it seemed so long ago. I wondered where Rusty was and what he might be doing. Well, at least I'll be seeing Julie again. I must write her. "Dear Julie, you'll never guess what has happened...." But on second thought, I might get back before she gets it.*

June July August September

September, 5

The time for leaving is drawing closer and closer. There are so many last-minute things to do. Some of them we can do right away. Our bikes, for instance. Dad took our bikes back to the dealer and he very kindly bought them from us. But of course, for less than we'd paid for them. Others things must wait until the very last minute. The movers will come the last day to pack our furniture for shipping. And before they arrived, we had to make sure all our things were packed. So we packed and packed and packed. It was really tiring. I realized we have lots more things now then when we arrived. It's surprising how much stuff* we'd acquired* over the summer. Mom started to pack my bathing suit in one of the boxes, but I wouldn't let her. "Why", she asked. "You won't need it for several months. Summer is still a long way off." "Please, Mom," I said. "It's so small I can carry it in my hand bag. Besides, I just want to have it with me. It makes me feel good." Just then Dad walked up. "Of course she does! That's Diane's good luck suit." Good old Dad. He always understands me.*

September, 6

(1)Well, today's the day. We're leaving. While Peter loads our suitcases into the car, Mom and I go through the rooms to make sure we haven't left anything behind. Then we lock the front door for the last time, and all of us get into the car. As we drive away for the last time, Peter and I strain to look back at our house. It looks so dark and silent. Maybe it's my imagination, but to me the house already looks sad, as if it hated to see us go. Dad leaves the house key off at the Real Estate Office. As we drive through the streets, I'm already starting to see them differently. I no longer belong here. I've become a stranger. A small part of me has already left. I half-expect to see my own self, riding bikes with my friends, coming down the street, carefree*. All my life I've wanted a bike. I wanted one in the worst way, more than anything else. Like all my friends and my swimming pool, it must be left behind. There's no place to ride in Taipei. When next summer comes I'm really going to miss our swimming pool. Isn't it funny how we think of things as "ours." Actually, we rent this house from someone else, so the pool really belongs to them, not me. But it's given me so much happiness and triumph*, in my heart it'll always be mine.*

June July August September

September, 6

(2)Father's friend, Mr. Johnson and his wife, have come down to the airport to see us off. Once again we step into the brisk air of San Francisco airport. Mr. Johnson and my father shake hands. "Well, David", he says. "I never thought we'd be saying goodbye so soon." "Neither did I," Dad answered with an ironic* smile. Mr. Johnson helps as we check our suitcases in at curb-side*. Then picking up our carry-on* bags, all of us push through the door. The night we arrived from Taiwan I couldn't tell how big the airport is. Wow, this place is huge! It's full of strangers, all about to fly off to different parts of the globe*. People all over the world will be waiting for them, looking at their clocks, counting the hours. Though they're still in San Francisco, their minds are already focused on where they're going. Sitting in the lounge*, looking outside, I can see lights on the hills, across the Bay. Just now, when I opened my handbag to look for something, I caught a glimpse of my bathing suit. Tears came to my eyes. I had to fight hard to keep them back.*

September, 6

(3)At last, we're sitting on the plane. The doors have just closed and locked with a thump. We're still in San Francisco, but I can feel Taiwan already reaching out to me, through the night, coming closer. It feels like my heart has rushed on ahead and already crossed some invisible line. Then with a mighty roar and a surge* of speed, our plane is in the air, circling. The lights of Berkeley and the East Bay gradually sink below us. Looking back, beyond the mountains, I can see a faint haze* of light in the deepening darkness of the Central Valley. That's where Claire and Melanie and all my friends are. Up until a few hours ago, that's where I lived, too. I wonder what Claire, Beatrice, Ruby, and the others are doing this moment? Probably finishing their homework and getting ready for bed. Will they ever pause in front of my house some evening, and miss me, as I miss them? I'd like to think they will, but, no, their lives are unchanged. Tomorrow they'll get up, go to school, ride their bikes, do their homework. If they remember me for anything, it'll be my little victories over Simon.*

The plane wheels. Stars overhead. We're going home.

5月31日

今天晚上，爸爸帶回一個令人興奮的消息。他的公司要調他到美國工作。我們全家都要跟他一起去。明年學校開學的時候，我會上美國的學校。我的同學都會是美國人。當然了，媽媽也很興奮，但是她也很擔心。爸爸叫她不要擔心，但一點都沒有用。媽媽是一個很實際的人，實際的人都擔心得太多。她擔心我要上哪種學校；擔心我的英文是否夠好；擔心要找一間好房子。爸爸說：「找房子不是問題。現在我們要想的是帶什麼東西過去。」我才不管這些事情呢。我太興奮了。吃完晚飯後，我們看了一個美國的電視節目。這個節目看起來跟以前不同，大概是因為我們就要去美國了。我知道今天晚上一定會睡不著。

生字表

transfer [træns`fɝ] v. 使調職
practical [`præktɪkḷ] adj. 實際的

6月1日

嗯，我說對了。我睡得不好。其實，我想昨天晚上大家都睡得不好，連哥哥都沒睡好。平常他怎麼樣都叫不醒，媽媽說就算是房子著火了，他也會一直睡下去。我可以聽見爸爸媽媽在說話，但是聽不清楚他們在說什麼；突然間，我清楚的聽到了。爸爸說：「也許我應該一個人去美國。」媽媽說：「那誰來照顧你呢？」爸爸回答：「也許就我們兩個人去，把孩子留在這裡。」媽媽想了一下說：「對，我們可以把他們留給你父母帶。」當我聽到這時就大聲叫：「不要！不要把我留下來，帶我一起去！」結果我睜開眼睛，發現這只是一個惡夢。我好高興喲！然後我看到房門口有個黑影。原來是哥哥彼得。我問他：「幹嘛？」彼得說：「你大喊大叫的，把我吵醒了。」我還一直以為他睡得跟豬一樣呢！我說：「喔！對不起。回去睡覺吧！」今晚真是漫漫長夜！連哥哥都睡不著。

生字表

catch on fire　著火
reply [rɪˋplaɪ] v. 回答
shadow [ˋʃædo] n. 影子
scream [skrim] v. 大聲喊叫

6月2日

今天是星期天，舅舅和舅媽過來吃中飯。當然了，我們聊的都是要去美國的事。舅媽非常支持我們去，她認為這是一個很棒的機會。她相信旅行對每個人來說一尤其是年輕人一是件好事。她說：「他們越年輕，就會從旅行中學得越多。我還在大學念書時，曾經在英國待了一個暑假，交了許多有趣的朋友，還到英國各地旅行，甚至還到歐洲做了一趟短程之旅。」她很高興的說著她的夏日旅行。「大學畢業後，我就開始工作了，接著結了婚。之後，就沒有機會再去旅行了。回想起來，在英國的那個夏天，是我這輩子最快樂的時光。」她嘆了一口氣。我看著舅舅。只要舅媽說到這件事，舅舅就一點笑容都沒有。

生字表

supportive [sə`pɔrtɪv] adj. 支持的
opportunity [,ɑpɚ`tjunətɪ] n. 機會
university [,junə`vɝsətɪ] n. 大學
graduate [`grædʒʊ,et] v. 畢業
sigh [saɪn] v. 嘆氣

6月3日

我要講一講我的舅舅。他是個奇怪的人。我當然很愛他，但是，說實在的，他有些想法很奇怪。他是媽媽的哥哥，也跟媽媽一樣很愛擔心。好像媽媽娘家的人都很愛擔心。但舅舅不只是愛擔心而已，他從來都看不到事情的光明面。他認為我們在美國會碰到可怕的事情。他說的話讓媽媽更擔心了。舅舅的問題出在他從來沒有出國旅行過，他認為出國旅行只是浪費錢而已。但是，我覺得他只是在嫉妒而已。他不信任外國人。只要電視在播美國電影，他就會說：「看看這些老外，他們簡直瘋了。」吃完午餐後，他告訴爸爸媽媽：「將來你們會失去女兒。她會嫁給外國人，到時候你們就見不到她了。」他說這句話時，連媽媽都笑了。她說：「我想我們還不用擔心這個，別忘了黛安才九歲。」就像我說的一樣，舅舅真的有點怪。

生字表

weird [wɪrd] adj. 奇怪的

6月 4日

6月
7月
8月
9月

距離出發的時間越來越近了。爸爸工作很忙，所以媽媽得決定要帶哪些東西走，和留哪些東西下來。晚上他們幾乎都是在講這件事情。忽然間，其他事情好像都不重要了。我看著我的朋友們過著普通的日子，雖然我人還在這裡，但我已經感覺和他們不一樣了。他們說很羨慕我，這可能是真的，但在某方面來說，我卻羨慕他們。他們永遠不會了解這一點。晚上想起要離開這裡的事情時，不像當初那麼令人興奮了。我沒辦法不這麼想。但每天太陽出來的時候，我總是覺得很有勇氣、很有自信，準備好好的面對未來。我問彼得會不會對離開這裡感到不安，他的回答很短，但一針見血：「為什麼？我們都會在一起呀！我們也會交到新的朋友，而且莎麗舅媽說美國是兒童的天堂。你有什麼好擔心的？」說的也對。我變得跟媽媽一樣了。

生字表

envy [ˋɛnvɪ] v. 羨慕，嫉妒
heaven [ˋhɛvən] n. 天堂

6月5日

今天下午我去莎麗舅媽家玩。我想聽聽更多有關住在國外的情形。有時候，我覺得她是我唯一可以談得來的人。她拿出相簿，給我看她在英國拍的相片。我已經看過這些照片幾百次了，但今天它們看起來和以前都不一樣，那是因為我用不同的眼光來看。照片裡的建築物看起來更漂亮，人看起來也不同了。我仔細的看這些人；我懷疑外星人就是長這個樣子。今天我跟舅媽說：「真不敢相信我要去這種地方。」舅媽回答說：「你才不會去這種地方。這些照片是在英國照的，你要去的是美國，這差別可大了。」我跟她說我不懂。我說：「他們都是講英文，怎麼可能會不一樣？」舅媽微笑著說：「等你長大可以旅行的時候，你就會知道了。」我想：「嘿！我來這是想很快得到一些解答，但我現在得帶著更多的疑問回家了！」

生字表

wonder [ˋwʌndɚ] v. 懷疑；想知道

6月6日

今天早上，媽媽說明天會有工人來裝運我們的東西，家裡會弄得一團亂，她不要我們在家以免礙事。我哀嚎著說：「那我們要去哪裡呢？」我好想哭。我們的世界好像漸漸的被顛倒過來了。哥哥說我是個愛哭鬼，但我知道他只是在裝酷，其實他的心裡跟我一樣擔心，只是他沒有表現出來而已。媽媽說我們要去和阿公阿媽住，一直到要出發的時候為止。她說這句話的時候，哥哥的眼睛瞪得好大。他一點都不酷了；他看起來很害怕。他看我的時候，我知道我們都在想同一件事：阿公阿媽住在鄉下，爸爸媽媽可能真的要自己去美國了。也許這就是他們要擺脫我們的方法？也許他們要自己去而把我們留下來？

生字表

shipping [ˋʃɪpɪŋ] n. 運送
mess [mɛs] n. 混亂
in the way 造成阻礙
wail [wel] v. 哀嚎著說
gradually [ˋgrædʒʊəlɪ] adv. 漸漸的
upside down 顛倒
pretend [prɪˋtɛnd] v. 假裝
get rid of 擺脫

6月7日

今天早上八點整，工人就準時按鈴了。他們吵吵鬧鬧的進來我們家，用鎚子和鋸子開始做木箱。砰！砰！砰！聲音真的好吵。一下子，我們家就變得跟戰場一樣。幸好我們昨晚就收好東西了。當我們要出門時，我回頭看看自己亂七八糟的房間，覺得很難過。我滿懷希望的問媽媽說我該不該留下來幫忙。她只摸摸我的頭，叫我動作快一點，但我想她知道我的感受。因為媽媽很忙，所以莎麗舅媽必須帶我們到阿公阿媽家。當火車頭轟隆隆的進站時，我們就上車去坐在我們的位子上。莎麗舅媽親切的對我們微笑，說：「打起精神來嘛！你們兩個看起來好像要去坐牢喔！你們一定會玩得很高興的。」然後火車就開動了。火車越開越快，一棟棟的房子都往後飛跑，但我太難過了，什麼事都沒注意到。我想念我自己的房間，但我最想念的是爸爸媽媽。我很害怕的問：「莎麗舅媽，他們不會把我們留下來，自己跑到美國去吧？」

生字表

exactly [ɪgˋzæktlɪ] adv. 準確地
saw [sɔ] n. 鋸子
crate [kret] n. 板條箱
pat [pæt] v. 輕拍
rumble [ˋrʌmbl̩] v. 發出隆隆聲
prison [ˋprɪzn̩] n. 監獄
flash [flæʃ] v. 快速閃過
battle field 戰場
my grandparents' = my grandparents' house 阿公阿媽家

6月8日

我們下午很晚才到。阿義伯父到車站接我們，他是爸爸的哥哥。平常他都騎摩托車，但今天我們人多，所以就搭公車到他們的村子。那個村子蠻遠的，坐公車快一個鐘頭才到。下車以後，還要坐當地的計程車才能到阿公阿媽的農莊。農莊就在山腳下，而且還蠻偏僻的。我們到的時候，天已經漸漸黑了，大家都在等我們一起吃飯。我快餓死了。吃過飯後，我和彼得在看電視。從阿公阿媽的談話中，我知道他們的想法和臺北人不一樣。他們不覺得去外國是件好事。他們說：「那麼遠。」其他人也說：「好危險喔。」星星在外面的天上閃閃發光。我在臺北從來沒有看過這麼多星星，我覺得我已經到了國外。後來我累得躺在沙發上睡著了。

生字表

foothill [ˋfʊtˏhɪl] n. 山腳下的小山丘
isolated [ˋaɪsl̩ˏetɪd] adj. 孤立的
starve [starv] v. 飢腸轆轆
pick up　接送

6月9日

今天早上，陽光照在臉上把我曬醒了。大家都不在。我躺在一張陌生的床上。我到底在哪裡？我聽到小鳥在唱歌。這種感覺好奇怪喔，我從來沒有在臺北聽過鳥叫，也許這是一場夢吧？我不覺得害怕，但是覺得很疑惑。慢慢的，我想起昨天的事情。從臺北坐火車，還有阿公阿媽，我記得我坐在沙發上，之後就不記得了。我睡著了以後，一定有人把我抱到這張床上。莎麗舅媽呢？彼得呢？我趕快起來穿好衣服。到客廳的時候，阿媽問說：「你肚子餓不餓？」說真的，我覺得很餓，但是外面有小孩子玩的聲音，我想去看他們在做什麼。一定是堂姊堂哥來了。我想趕快出去跟他們一起玩。我聽到彼得的聲音，就知道他們玩得很高興。誰要吃飯？我已經浪費太多時間了。我要出去跟他們一起玩，一分鐘都不要等！

6月
7月
8月
9月

6月10日

今天天氣好熱。彼得說良松堂哥要帶我們去一個地方玩。良松堂哥是彼得的死黨，只要我們在鄉下，如果你看到良松堂哥，彼得一定就在他左右。良松說：「我們去捉蝦子吧！」然後我們就出發了。我們很興奮的跟著他。他帶我們到附近一條很清澈的小溪，裡面有很多的蝦子。一路上，我們碰到他好幾個朋友。這個地方房子不是很多，小孩倒是多得很。每碰到一個他的朋友，良松就邀請他跟我們去捉蝦，沒有人拒絕。他們知道我們是臺北來的，所以對我們很好奇。我覺得有點不好意思，因為裡面只有彼得和我是穿著鞋子的。他們都光著腳丫子。我想把鞋子脫掉，但是小路上的鵝卵石好燙，我的腳被燙得好痛，我只好再把鞋穿上。到了小溪的時候，我趕快把腳泡到水裡，感覺真舒服。你知道捉蝦子的時候，牠們都會往後跳嗎？我本來不知道，但我現在知道了。

生字表

embarrassed [ɪm`bærəst] adj. 尷尬的
barefoot [`bɛr,fʊt] adj. 赤腳的
pebble [`pɛbl̩] n. 鵝卵石

6月11日

今天真的好刺激喔！阿媽在客廳看到一條蛇，盤在一張竹椅下面。阿公阿媽的房子是在山上，夏天的時候，蛇就成了這裡的問題。即使在最熱的日子裡，高高的天花板也會讓屋子保持涼快；但不巧的是蛇喜歡涼快的房子，他們會爬進來避暑。今天我們在房子前面玩的時候，突然聽到阿媽叫了一聲。我們趕快跑進去。我簡直不敢相信我的眼睛！有一隻好大、看起來很兇惡的蛇盤在一張椅子下面。阿公把牠從房子裡趕走，我問他為什麼不把牠殺掉，他說：「蛇都有自己的伴，如果你殺了一條，另外一條會來找牠。我們可不要另外一條蛇跑到房子裡來。」後來我跟阿媽說，好險是她發現這條蛇。我說：「如果是我的話，我一定會心臟病發。」阿媽說：「別胡說，小孩子才不會心臟病發。」慘了，我想今天晚上我會睡不著覺。

生字表

coil [kɔɪl] v. 盤繞
bamboo [bæm`bu] n. 竹子
unfortunately [ʌn`fɔrtʃənɪtlɪ] adv. 不湊巧的
crawl [krɔl] vi. 爬行
escape [ə`skep] vt. 逃避
mate [met] n. 同伴
heart attack 心臟病發

6月 12日

我猜的沒錯，昨晚花了好長的時間才睡著。我一直聽到奇怪的聲音，是蛇。我確定這個聲音是從床下傳出來的！我可以想像有條蛇盤在我的床下面，等我下床的時候咬我一口。萬一牠爬上床怎麼辦？我用毯子把自己從頭到腳包起來。雖然晚上很熱，但這樣我覺得比較安全一點。早上醒來的時候，我偷偷看看床邊，先確定沒有蛇在那裡等我。我跟阿公說這件事，他叫我別擔心。他說：「蛇在晚上獵食，晚上比較涼，所以牠們才會在那時候獵食。牠們晚上對房子沒有興趣，但是在白天的時候，牠們偶爾會爬進房子來避暑。」阿公的話讓我覺得好過一點。每天晚上，我們都會把竹椅搬到外面，在黑暗中聊天、看星星。外面很涼爽。我就這樣在夜晚的星空下睡著了。

生字表

peek [piːk] vi. 偷瞄
edge [ɛdʒ] n. 邊緣

6月 13日

今天早上，良松堂哥跟他妹妹小萍帶我們去捉蝸牛。良松的工作是餵他家的鴨子。他們說鴨子愛吃蝸牛，所以找我們去幫忙捉。在又濕又涼的地方可以找到蝸牛，而蛇也喜歡這種地方，所以我們得小心。良松堂哥帶來了一根棍子先打草驚蛇，然後我們就開始進去捉蝸牛了。我跟彼得都找不到牠們，於是良松和小萍教我們該往哪裡找。我們把所有的蝸牛放在一個袋子裡，然後回堂哥堂姊的家。良松拿了一把大菜刀，然後「砰！」「砰！」幾聲，把所有的蝸牛拍成黏黏的肉醬，真的好噁心喔！但我想如果你是一隻鴨子的話，就會覺得很好吃吧！回家的時候，下起了一場大雨，良松趕快摘了幾張大葉子給我們遮雨。我們用手抓著葉子的莖，把葉子當做傘來撐。到家的時候，我們全身都濕了。我從來沒在下雨的時候，玩得這麼開心過。

生字表

whack [hwæk] vi. 用力劈打
gooey [`guɪ] adj. 黏稠的
disgusting [dɪs`gʌstɪŋ] adj. 噁心的
stalk [stɔk] n. 莖，葉柄

6月 14日

今天發生了一件很好笑的事，到現在，只要我想到這件事，就會又笑出來。今天彼得失蹤了，聽起來好像很神祕，對不對？我們有半個鐘頭找不到他的人影。本來他在追良松，他們兩個人嘻嘻哈哈的跑到房子後面的山坡上。一會兒，良松一個人回來了。小萍和我問：「彼得呢？」良松說：「他就在後面。」我們等了又等，但是還是不見彼得的人影。良松說：「他可能躲在外面吧。」但我不這麼想。他到底會在哪裡啊？我們開始去找他。我們找遍了屋子後面，叫著他的名字，但是都沒有回答。然後我們聽到一個微弱的聲音：「救命啊！救命啊！我在這邊！」我們就跑過去看。彼得掉到糞坑裡了！我們都開始大笑，連哥哥自己也在笑。他爬不出來，所以我們得幫忙把他拉上來。他全身髒兮兮的，阿媽要用水管沖他，才能把那些糞沖走。這裡真好玩！我永遠都不想走。

生字表

mysterious [mɪs`tɪrɪəs] adj. 不可思議的
slope [slop] n. 斜坡
giggle [`gɪgḷ] vi. 咯咯的笑
cesspool [`sɛs,pul] n. 糞坑
filth [fɪlθ] n. 污物
hose [hoz] n. 水管

6月15日

今天晚上，叔叔說他要到商店去買點東西，叫我跟他一起去。到那裡要走二十分鐘。我想我要先談談我叔叔。雖然他已經二十歲了，但他還像個小孩一樣。我們走回家的時候，他忽然說：「等一下，我看到那棵樹下有鬼！」我尖叫了起來。如果你曾經在晚上的時候待在鄉下，而且有人跟你說他們看到了鬼，你就知道我有多害怕。我把臉蒙起來，一點都不敢看，要是你的話你敢看嗎？叔叔聽起來很害怕的說：「我們前面還有一個，後面也來了一個！」他大聲叫說：「我們趕快跑！」他抓住我的手，我們就跑了起來。我一路都大聲尖叫，我確定那個鬼隨時都會抓到我。我們到家的時候，叔叔倒在地上大笑。原來這只是個玩笑而已。但是這是個很成功的玩笑，所以我不生氣，一點都不氣。當時在黑暗中，叔叔聽起來真的很害怕。他可以當個很棒的電影明星了。我在這裡玩得好開心喔！誰有這個福氣有這麼好玩的叔叔？

生字表

ought to　應該
grab [græb] vt. 抓住

6月16日

早上阿公說我們明天就要走了，所以今天是我們待在這裡的最後一天。吃完晚飯後叔叔說：「今天晚上很特別，我們來放沖天砲吧！」我們大喊：「好啊，好啊，我們來玩！」當叔叔出來的時候，我們都圍在他旁邊。叔叔把一個沖天砲放在地上，然後把它點燃。它爆炸的時候，發出了「砰」的一聲巨響，我們都歡呼了起來。然後他把另一個沖天砲放在一個鐵罐下面，把它點燃，鐵罐就被炸到空中。「叔叔，讓我點一個。」堂哥堂姊開始等得有點不耐煩，但叔叔還在找其他的東西來炸。他看了看家裡的貓，那隻貓馬上跳起來逃走了，速度快得跟閃電一樣。狗很不安的看著叔叔，並搖搖牠的尾巴。彼得求他說：「拜託啦，叔叔，讓我們玩吧！」「你們太小了，可能會受傷。」我們這才知道，叔叔玩得那麼開心，他才不想停下來呢。我覺得我好像一直都住在這裡，臺北似乎離我好遠。美國呢？天啊，聽起來好像是外星球一樣。

生字表

firecracker [`faɪr,krækɚ] n. 炮竹
explode [ɪk`splod] vi. 爆炸
wag [wæg] vt. 擺動
beg [bɛg] vi. 懇求
planet [`plænɪt] n. 行星

6月17日

今天該走了。我的一個叔叔會帶我們到機場去。我很想再看到爸爸媽媽，但我不想離開阿公阿媽。早上我幾乎沒辦法穿上鞋子。我光著腳丫子跑來跑去太久了，穿鞋子覺得很不舒服，鞋子穿起來好緊。堂哥堂姊還有其他的小孩都來和我們說再見，他們都不說話，不像平常一樣，會大聲的計畫今天有什麼活動。良松堂哥送我一個禮物，他說：「這樣你就不會忘記我們。」他用葉子做了一隻蚱蜢。美國的生活會不會像鄉下這裡一樣刺激？沒有堂哥堂姊，沒有愛玩的叔叔，沒有蛇，沒有蝸牛，沒有鴨子。我們往外走的時候，我回頭看他們，大家都站在那裡跟我們揮手。我會想念阿媽的。我們一上公車，彼得就睡著了。真是本性難移，一點感情都沒有。唉，去桃園中正機場怎麼要坐這麼久的車呢？

生字表

grasshopper [ˋgræs,hɑpɚ] n. 蚱蜢
fashion [ˋfæʃən] vt. 做成…的形狀

6月18日

我現在在飛機上寫這篇日記。不知道現在是幾點。不知道現在是今天還是已經過了一天。我們已經起飛很久了，但窗外還是黑黑的。我們到機場的時候，爸爸媽媽就站在機場外面等。我們好高興看到他們。我們一定是有點遲到了，因為他們看起來有一點擔心。我們一到機場就一起上二樓去，然後通過一道門，那裡有些穿制服的人在檢查護照。再往裡面一點的地方，有人檢查我們隨身攜帶的包包。等到了候機室時，已經有人開始上飛機了。彼得說開始坐飛機的時候，他先讓我坐靠窗口的位置，媽媽坐在中間，就在我旁邊。忽然有一陣好大的轟隆聲，隨著一陣衝力，飛機就往前衝，然後飛上了天空。我從黑漆漆的窗外往下看，可以看到小小的燈光。不知道其中有沒有一個燈光是我阿公阿媽家的。

生字表

passport [ˋpæs,port] n. 護照
roar [ror] n. 轟隆聲

6月19日

我剛醒過來，不知道今天是幾號，也不知道我在那裡。我們在空中的某個地方，很強的陽光從窗口射進來。阿公阿媽的家還有堂哥堂姊感覺上離我好遠。彼得說飛機起飛的時候我可以先坐靠窗的位置，但要下降的時候，就要把位子還他，現在我知道為什麼了。原來根本沒東西可看，只有一層像地毯的雲。我覺得我被騙了。媽媽說我們正在海洋的上空，我想看看海或是船，但是什麼都看不到。爸爸和媽媽今天早上看起來不太好，不知道為什麼，他們看起來跟以前不一樣。他們一樣是他們，但又有點不一樣。可能他們睡得不好吧。我也睡得不好，但彼得就跟平常一樣，一點都沒有被干擾，睡得很熟。當他們宣布我們快到舊金山時，彼得要我把靠窗的位子讓給他。當我們飛過加州海岸線時，我可以看到一點點綠色的山。現在我們準備降落了，我不能再寫了。

生字表

bother [`bɑðɚ] vt. 使煩惱
announce [ə`nauns] vt. 宣布，通知
approach [ə`protʃ] vt. 接近，即將到達
glimpse [glɪmps] n. 一瞥

6月19日

（同一天，晚上十一點三十分）

趁關燈以前還有一點時間，我來寫一點東西。今天晚上真忙。飛機停在下機門之後，所有的乘客就開始穿上他們的外套，把放在頭上行李艙裡的行李拿下來。在這之前，大家不是在睡覺就是看起來很無聊，但是忽然之間，大家都變得很忙。當機艙門打開的時候，大家開始走得很快，有些人幾乎是用跑的。我問爸爸為什麼，他說也許外面有人在等他們。我們得大排長龍等著檢查護照。那個移民局官員看起來不太友善。他問了一些問題之後，就在我們的護照上蓋了章。我們拿了行李後就走到迎客區，爸爸公司裡的強森先生在那裡等我們，我們在前面入口處等他去把車子開過來。現在天已經黑了，而且晚上的空氣很涼。我覺得有一股莫名的興奮。接著強森先生開了車子過來，我們就上車了。我們到美國了。

生字表

overhead [`ovɚ,hɛd] adj. 頭頂的
immigration [,ɪmə`greʃən] n. 移居，移民
suitcase [`sut,kes] n. 行李箱
chilly [`ʧɪlɪ] adj. 冰冷的

6月20日

這是我們在美國的第一個早晨。我醒來的時候，爸爸已經到公司去了。我從柔軟的床上爬起來，走過柔軟的地毯把窗簾拉開。外面，二十層樓下，就是舊金山。在明亮的日光照耀下，沒想到舊金山看起來是那麼的美麗。我可以看到海灣、橋、以及在它們後面的山。舊金山比我想像的還漂亮！彼得和我興奮的在房間裡跳來跳去，叫媽媽快一點。舊金山在等著我們呢！我們到走廊時，柔軟的地毯和空無一人的走廊真是個大誘惑！彼得和我沿著走廊跑，看誰先按到電梯的按鈕。媽媽罵我們說：「你們兩個乖一點，如果經理看到你們這樣跑來跑去，我們會被趕出去的。」我們在外面的天空和陽光下走了一會兒，但很快就覺得累了，不知道為什麼會這樣。媽媽說是因為時差的關係。我們的身體還在臺灣的時間，也就是差不多凌晨兩點。我們的身體在告訴我們它們要睡覺。

生字表

story [`storɪ] n. 樓層
bay [be] n. 海灣
corridor [`kɔrədɚ] n. 迴廊
temptation [tɛmp`teʃən] n. 誘惑
button [`bʌtn̩] n. 按鈕
sharply [`ʃɑrplɪ] adv. 嚴厲的
jet lag 時差

6月
7月
8月
9月

6月21日

今天是星期天。早上爸爸說吃完晚餐後，就要離開舊金山，開車到加州中部的一個小鎮。我們會在那裡住一年。中午我們就退了房，把行李交給旅館保管。雖然星期天在美國是假日，可是在我們離開前，爸爸還有很多事要做。他說五點半的時候會在旅館和我們會合。他走了以後，我們三個人—媽媽、彼得和我—站在旅館外面商量著要到哪裡去。每個方向看起來都很吸引人。在一邊，「加州街」往下延伸到中國城去，但我們對中國城沒有興趣，我們才剛從臺灣來，要看點不同的東西，所以就往「聯合廣場」走去。走到「鮑爾街」轉角時，我們很驚訝的停了下來。沒想到街道居然那麼的陡！回到旅館的時候，爸爸已經在那裡等我們了。我們在出發前吃了晚餐。吃飯時，大家都顯得異常的安靜。時差還是影響著我們。

生字表

inviting [ɪnˋvaɪtɪŋ] adj. 吸引人的
descend [dɪˋsɛnd] vi. 下降
steep [stip] adj. 陡峭的

6月22日

今天早上吃早餐前，我和彼得散了一下步。我們住在火車站旁的一個小旅館。這間旅館和舊金山那間不一樣，舊金山的旅館非常高雅，但這個旅館很整潔、感覺很親切，就跟這個小鎮一樣。昨晚我們很晚才到，在開車來的路上，我發現美國真的好大好大！你要親眼看到才能了解。太平洋也很大，但飛機飛得很高，你感覺不到。在地圖上，這個小鎮離舊金山只有兩吋遠。我想：「很近嘛！」但我們卻花了好幾個鐘頭開車才到這裡！出發之後，我很快就睡著了。醒來的時候，我們還沒到。我們在空曠的黑暗裡一直開，沒有路標、沒有其他的車，四週只有好幾哩遠的黑暗。偶爾會在遠方有一些小小的燈光，可能是個孤立的農舍，接著好幾哩路又是一片黑暗。我想告訴爸爸我的感覺，但是我太累了。媽媽說我們到了之後，他們費了好大的勁才把我叫醒。

生字表

elegant [`ɛləgənt] adj. 雅緻的
neat [nit] adj. 整潔的
Pacific Ocean 太平洋

6月23日

今天我們要去找房子。爸爸昨天跟一位房屋仲介商約好了。他說：「我們要找房子，不想浪費時間。」爸爸說住旅館對小孩子不好。我知道彼得喜歡住在旅館，這樣他就不用清理房間了。我跟爸爸一樣，希望趕快安頓下來。我想要有自己的房間，然後把所有的東西都放在我身邊。吃完早餐後，仲介商在旅館大廳和我們會合。她的名字是巴恩司太太。爸爸已經解釋過我們需要哪一種房子，所以巴恩司太太準備了一張名單，列出幾間她認為我們會喜歡的房子。巴恩司太太有自己的車，我們當然也有一部租來的車，可是兩部車都不夠大，無法載我們全部的人。巴恩司太太問：「誰要跟我坐同一部車呢？」媽媽說她要跟她坐。我想過要坐她的車，因為她看起來人很好，可是我只會幾個英文字，萬一她開始和我說話怎麼辦？我一定會丟臉死了。

生字表

appointment [ə`pɔɪntmənt] n. 約定會面
real estate 不動產
agent [`edʒənt] n. 代理人，仲介
settle down 定居
lobby [`lɑbɪ] n.（旅館）大廳

6月24日

我們整整兩天都在找房子。它們都好漂亮，就像美國電影裡的那些房子一樣。在美國電影裡的小孩子似乎都住在漂亮的房子裡，而很快的，我們也會住在裡面。媽媽、彼得和我都決定不了那一間最好，爸爸則是什麼都沒說。爸爸有個特點，就是每當要做決定的時候，他都會馬上決定。做決定對他來說一點問題都沒有，而且他每次做的決定，也似乎都是對的。也許這就是為什麼他在公司有這麼重要的地位吧！爸爸不是那種事情需要考慮好幾天的人。媽媽有點不同。在這方面，彼得比較像爸爸，但有時候也會像媽媽，我則是比較像媽媽。我們看的房子都有漂亮的院子、大廚房、可以停兩部車的車庫、而且至少有三個房間。唯一的不同似乎是它們的大小。有些房子的院子比較大，有些房子的房間比較多。我很喜歡看這些漂亮的房子。真希望明天趕快來。

生字表

take after　與…相似
look forward to　期待

6月25日

6月
7月
8月
9月

早上吃完早餐後，爸爸告訴我們：「不用再找房子了，我們已經看夠了。」我和彼得都沒說話，看他接下來要說什麼。「昨晚你媽媽和我談過了，我們決定了麥克丹尼爾大道的房子是最合適的。」麥克丹尼爾大道？彼得和我只記得地方和東西的樣子，名字對我們來說沒什麼意義。我們分不出這個英文稱呼和那個英文稱呼的差別。吃完早餐後，我們到仲介商的辦公室去，爸爸簽了租約，然後巴恩司太太把鑰匙交給我們，我們就開車到新家去了。今天，我們看這間房子的眼光變得不一樣了。從現在開始，起碼會有一年的時間，它會是我們的房子，那會讓你看事情的眼光有所不同。它看起來甚至比以前更棒：房子靠近人行道，所以前院小一點，但是後院則是又深又寬，有塊大片的草地，被樹和矮叢圍繞。最棒的是，那裡有個游泳池！你能想像嗎？我們自己的游泳池耶！今年夏天會是我這輩子最快樂的夏天了！

生字表

avenue [`ævə͵nu] n. 大道，大街
lease [lis] n. 租約
lawn [lɔn] n. 草坪
border [`bɔrdɚ] vt. 圍住
shrub [ʃrʌb] n. 矮樹叢
entire [ɪn`taɪr] adj. 整個的

6月26日

今早我們從旅館退房，搬進我們的新家。這間房子就是美國人說的「帶部分家具的房子」，這表示房子裡有家具、洗衣機、冰箱和爐子，可是不包括布類製品，所以我們早上去買了床單、毯子、枕頭套和毛巾，之後又到市場去買肥皂和浴室用品。我以為我們會買菜，但是爸爸說：「不行，我們還有別的事要先做。」吃過午餐後，我們送媽媽回家。她要整理床鋪，開始將房子裡的一切準備就緒。然後爸爸開車到一個很大的公園去。它比臺北的什麼地方都大，草和樹都很乾淨、整齊，在藍色的天空下，延伸了幾條街那麼遠！光是看到它，就讓我想脫下鞋子奔跑，或者是追彼得，或者是躺在草地上。我們進入了一棟在樹間的矮建築物，爸爸跟桌子後面一位年輕的小姐說話。她往我這裡看來，而且對我微笑。她的眼神很親切而且閃閃發光。我們的眼神交會時，我馬上就喜歡上她了。

生字表

check out　結帳離開
furnish [ˋfɝnɪʃ] vt. 設置家俱
linen [ˋlɪnən] n. 亞麻布製品（如床單，桌巾等）
pillowcase [ˋpɪlo͵kes] n. 枕頭套
article [ˋartɪkl̩] n. 物品
make the bed　鋪床
stretch [strɛtʃ] vt. 延伸，綿延
twinkling [ˋtwɪŋklɪŋ] adj. 閃亮的

6月27日

今早媽媽告訴我們：「今天我們要去超市和商店買菜。從現在起，我們要在家裡吃飯。」我想：「太棒了，現在可以看到美國超市裡面長什麼樣子了。」我們到的時候，彼得說：「哇，媽，這個地方真大！」那裡有一堆一堆的新鮮蔬菜和水果，我只認出幾樣而已。裡面有一排排我在臺北從沒看過的東西。這家店很大，大到我們跟彼得走散了好幾次。他自己走開了，我們都找不到他。我們也買了一個「炒菜鍋」。媽媽說：「我不會用美國的平底鍋煮菜，如果一定得用美國平底鍋的話，我們可能會餓死。」那天晚上，我們第一次吃了在美國自己家裡煮的菜。說實在的，菜不怎麼好吃。媽媽說她不知道怎麼控制電爐的熱度，結果她把魚燒焦了，可是我們不在意。其實，我們都笑了。在吃了一星期的旅館及餐廳的食物之後，那條燒焦的魚吃起來很香。

生字表

row [ro] n. 排
wander [`wandɚ] vi. 漫遊，閒逛
wok [wak] n. 有手把的中國炒菜鍋

6月28日

今天是星期日，爸爸一大早就告訴我們壞消息。他幫我們報名參加了夏令營。這就是那天他在公園裡辦的事。彼得看著我，我馬上就知道他在想什麼。我們兩個只會講幾個英文字。彼得看起來很擔心，我想我看起來也一樣。不管怎麼樣，我真的覺得很擔心。爸爸看到我們的表情就笑著說:「高興一點嘛，別那麼難過！你們會跟其他小朋友在一起，一定會玩得很開心的。星期五和我說話的女孩就是活動負責人，她是大學生。她說語言不是問題，你們這種年紀的孩子學得很快。她說的沒錯，我打賭等九月開學的時候，你們兩個的英文就會說得不錯了。」我一句話都沒說。我知道他是好意，而且在試著鼓勵我們，只是我心裡並不相信他的話。我會的英文只有「Hi」還有「Hello」，而且媽媽告訴我說，連我的「Hello」聽起來也有點怪怪的。她說聽起來像是「蛤摟」。

生字表

sign up for　報名參加
bet [bɛt] vt. 打賭
encourage [ɪn`kɝɪdʒ] vt. 鼓勵

6月29日

我累得幾乎一動也不能動。今天是夏令營的第一天。經過一整天的遊戲跟活動、再加上緊張，使得我全身酸痛。我們星期五看到的那位很好的小姐帶我們到教室去。因為彼得年紀比較大，他被分到不同的組去。當彼得去他的教室時，我覺得有點孤單。我可以聽到旁邊的教室傳出小朋友的笑聲和說話聲。夏令營已經開始一個星期了，所以所有的小孩子都已經互相認識。老師說：「來吧，黛安，我們去見其他的小朋友。」進到教室的時候，大家都轉頭看我們，我覺得很害羞。老師說：「今天來了一個新朋友，黛安一家人上星期才搬到我們鎮上，我們大家來歡迎她。」所有的小朋友都微笑著大喊：「嗨，黛安！」他們對我很好，但我沒辦法跟他們溝通，也聽不懂人家說什麼。好險今天的活動很簡單，我就跟著其他的小朋友一起做。不過雖然是這樣，我還是出了點錯。我明天要怎麼過啊？

生字表

ache [ek] vi.（持續的）疼痛
get through　撐過

6月30日

早上老師給我們做一個美勞作業，我覺得很簡單也很有趣。坐我旁邊的女孩慢慢的做給我看，所以我可以跟著她做。她叫我黛安，可是我會的英文很少，不知道怎麼問她的名字，所以我只能微笑。吃過午餐後，班上同學玩了一些遊戲，但我不知道應該做什麼。老師對我很好，他說：「黛安，我們兩個到這裡坐下來。大家玩遊戲的時候，我們可以聊一聊。」我們在草地上坐下來，他問我一些家裡的事，都是些很簡單的問題。他問我有沒有兄弟姐妹？我只會回答：「是」或「不是」。我想他好像有問到爸爸是做什麼的，可是我不確定。跟一個不會回答的人說話一定很無聊。到了回家的時間，他又跟我說話。我微笑說：「好。」希望我做對了。不管怎樣，他就點頭說：「好，明天見。」不知道他說了什麼。唉！大概不是什麼重要的事吧。但願如此。

生字表

be supposed to　應該

7月1日

今天早上，我發現每個小朋友都帶了個包包。我是唯一沒有包包的人，這讓我有點緊張。然後，吃完午餐後，老師說：「好，各位小朋友，游泳的時間到了！」我聽不懂他說什麼，但他一定是這麼說，因為所有的小孩都歡呼著往門外衝，我則是跟在他們後面。有些小孩一路都用跑的。有個被樹圍繞的室外游泳池在附近。我們到的時候，所有小孩子都衝到更衣室去換衣服，那時我才知道那些包包裡是什麼。它們就是游泳衣和毛巾。老師看看我，但他沒有說話。他昨天就是試著跟我說這件事。所有人都很快的跳下水，又潛水、又潑水，笑得很開心。他們玩得好高興。我躺在游泳池邊的椅子上看著天空，藍色的天空一片雲都沒有。今天是適合游泳的好日子，而只有我一個人沒帶泳衣。

生字表

dive [daɪv] vi. 跳水
splash [splæʃ] vi. 激起水花

7月2日

就某方面來說，也許昨天沒帶泳衣是件好事。我注意到其他人穿的泳衣和我的不一樣。我說不上來哪裡不同，但它們就是不一樣，男生女生穿的都是。昨晚寫完日記後，我把泳衣翻出來看。在臺灣它看起來還可以，但現在它看起來不太對勁。泳衣的樣式不對，顏色也似乎太鮮豔了。在夏令營，大家穿的泳衣顏色都比較柔和。我跟媽媽解釋這個問題，我知道她認為這樣很浪費，但她說要問問爸爸。爸爸了解我的想法，他說：「小孩討厭跟別人不一樣，彼得跟黛安因為不會講英文，已經覺得跟別人不一樣了，如果買件泳衣可以讓她更適應一點的話，那就買給她好了。」沒人比爸爸更了解我。所以今天我從夏令營回來時，媽媽跟我就到店裡去看泳衣。我選了一件確定錯不了的泳衣，真等不及要穿它了。

生字表

fit in　適應
by all means　一定

6月
7月
8月
9月

7月3日

我們有四個不同的指導老師或領隊，早上有兩個，下午則是另外兩個。他們都很年輕。但那是爸爸說的，對我來說他們看起來都好老。他們每一個人從小就住在這個小鎮，甚至在我們這個年紀的時候，也參加了這個夏季活動。我覺得這很有趣。美國這麼大，又很容易到處旅行，但他們都喜歡這個小鎮，一直沒有搬到別的地方去。「鐵鏽」是我們下午的一位領隊，他就是星期二跟我一起坐下來說話的老師。雖然他知道我聽不太懂英文，但過去這兩天他都過來跟我說了一會兒的話。他告訴我大家叫他「鐵鏽」是因為他小時候頭髮的顏色很紅，就像鐵鏽的顏色一樣。「鐵鏽」是大學生，秋天學校開學時，他就升大四了。他畢業以後要當老師。我希望這裡的學校開學時，我的新老師會跟「鐵鏽」一樣好。

生字表

instructor [ɪn`strʌktɚ] n. 指導老師
attend [ə`tɛnd] vt. 參加
reddish [`rɛdɪʃ] adj. 淡紅色的
rust [rʌst] n. 鐵鏽

7月4日

終於，今天可以休息了。不用擔心聽不懂別人說的話，不用擔心會做錯事。今天是七月四日，美國的獨立紀念日，所以放假一天，爸爸不用去上班。快中午的時候，我們開車到大學商場去，媽媽要買些下星期要用的東西。我們報名參加夏令營的時候，每個人都發到一件 T 恤，前面橫寫著「歡樂夏令營」的字樣。我看到一群女孩子穿著夏令營的 T 恤，但我一個都不認識。她們是別班的學生吧。真的是別班的嗎？其實我不能確定。我也穿了我的 T 恤，後來，這群人走過來的時候，她們跟我說：「嗨！」，但我不認識她們。爸爸說：「看到了吧？妳很快就會有很多的新朋友。」我跟他說，如果不會講英文的話，我永遠都交不到朋友。爸爸微笑著說：「等著瞧，妳會明白我的意思。」

生字表

enroll [ɪn`rol] vi. 登記
recognize [`rɛkəg,naɪz] vt. 認出

6月
7月
8月
9月

7月5日

我天天都在練習游泳。我們剛搬來這間房子的時候，我只會狗爬式。星期三的時候，我發現大部分的小朋友都很會游泳；事實上，有些人游得非常棒。所以，我下定決心要學會游泳。不只是會游，而且要游得好。我大概永遠都學不會講英文，但既然家裡後院有個游泳池，我的泳技一定會變好。在買新泳衣的那一天，我就開始練習了。現在我已經有點進步了，雖然不是很多，但是多少有點進展。今晚爸爸幫助我練習。爸爸是一流的游泳健將，他跟我說只要放輕鬆就好。「把水當做妳的朋友，」他說，「跟它合作。不管妳要怎麼做，就是不要抵抗它。」他教我怎麼用腿把自己推到池子中間。爸爸不注意的時候，彼得就嘲笑我。我知道他想把我的頭壓到水裡去，可是他不敢，他知道我會尖叫，何況，他自己也不太會游。我們等著瞧，看看一個星期後，是誰壓誰的頭下水。

生字表

dog-paddle [`dɔg,pædḷ] vi. 狗爬式游泳
make up one's mind 下定決心
certainly [`sɝtənlɪ] adv. 一定
relax [rɪ`læks] vi. 放鬆
duck [dʌk] vt. 將…按入水中
dare [dɛr] vi. 敢

7月6日

每次我們去買東西的時候，我跟彼得都不用擔心付錢的事。那跟我們沒關係。媽媽或爸爸在付錢時，我們都在隨便亂逛。我不會數美金，彼得也不會。今天晚上，爸爸從口袋裡掏出一些硬幣放在桌上，他說：「我們現在住在美國，所以你們要學會用美金。你們知不知道這裡每個硬幣的價值呢？」我們仔細的看了看，但是當然不知道它們的價值。爸爸拿起一個銅幣然後說：「這是一分，值一分錢。」然後他指著最小的一個硬幣說：「這是一角，值十分錢。」接下來一個小時，我們就練習辨認一分、五分、一角、和二十五分。起先，我們認得有點慢，但很快我們就會了。最後，在爸爸用一些問題測驗我們後，他說：「好，星期天帶你們到消費合作社去練習一下，看你們怎麼用美金。」到星期天還很久，我怕我在這段時間內就什麼都忘記了。

生字表

copper [ˋkɑpɚ] adj. 銅的
penny [ˋpɛnɪ] n. 一分硬幣
dime [daɪm] n. 一角硬幣
identify [aɪˋdɛntəˏfaɪ] vt. 辨認
nickel [ˋnɪkl̩] n. 五分鎳幣
quarter [ˋkwɔrtɚ] n. 二十五分硬幣
catch on　明白
co-op [koˋɑp] n. 消費合作社
in the meantime　同時

7月7日

在夏令營的第一個星期，因為我很害羞，所以沒有注意有那些人在我的班上。現在我覺得自在多了，但我還是分不出來誰是誰。就某方面來說，這有點像是學數美金一樣，只是這個比較難一點。認硬幣簡單，認臉就要花點時間了，至少我們班上同學的臉要花點時間才能認出來。今天瑪拉老師叫我把蠟筆發給全班同學。我拿了蠟筆在教室走了一圈，發給每個人一些。走到最後一排的時候，我猶豫了一下。第一個女生看起來很面熟，我不確定是不是已經發過蠟筆給她。她的桌上沒有蠟筆；我很沒把握。那個女生笑著說：「我是卡洛，妳剛才給過我妹妹蠟筆。」她指著一個第一排的女生，然後又說：「別難過，很多人都會把我們搞混。」我笑著把蠟筆分給她，但我心裡面想：「怎麼辦？班上的女生看起來都像姊妹一樣！」夏令營還有七個禮拜，我一定撐不下去。

生字表

tell...apart　分辨
crayon [`kreən] n. 蠟筆
hesitate [`hɛzə,tet] vi. 遲疑
familiar [fə`mɪljɚ] adj. 熟悉的
mix up　混淆

7月8日

跟其他同學一起游泳的確比自己一個人游泳有趣。我喜歡有自己的游泳池，但感覺跟和其他人在一起的時候不同。在家裡游泳是很安靜、很平靜的一起碼彼得不在的時候是這樣。也許那是因為我在家都是一個人在傍晚時游泳吧。我很努力練習。對我來說，在家游泳是比較嚴肅的，家裡院子的游泳池從來沒有像今天社區中心的游泳池那麼好玩過。天空跟上星期一樣的晴朗，可是這次我穿了我的新泳衣，就跟其他人一起跳進了游泳池。真是不可思議！男生馬上就佔了泳池深水區那一邊，他們追來追去，在池裡又跳水、又爬上岸。女生就自己玩自己的；有些人潛水看誰先找到水裡的硬幣—我認出來那是個兩毛五的硬幣。我跟其他人在水淺的一邊玩水。今晚我全身又僵硬又疲累。我的皮膚被太陽曬得連躺下來都覺得痛。今天真好玩。

生字表

a bunch of　一群
community [kə`mjunətɪ] n. 社區
unbelievable [͵ʌnbɪ`livəbl̩] adj. 不可思議的
immediately [ɪ`midɪɪtlɪ] adv. 立刻
shallow [`ʃælo] adj. 淺的
stiff [stɪf] adj. 僵直不動的
sunburned [`sʌn͵bɝnd] adj. 曬傷的

7月9日

到目前為止，夏令營裡玩的遊戲都有點難。對我來說很難，不過對班上其他人來說就不會了。遊戲難的原因就是因為我不會說英文，但今天玩的是我不用說話的遊戲。這遊戲不但玩起來好玩，看別人玩也很有趣。一開始當瑪拉告訴我們要練習寫自己名字時，大家都覺得很失望。他們抱怨說：「拜託，瑪拉，這個不好玩，太簡單了。」但他們錯了。寫自己的名字應該很簡單，但用瑪拉要求的方法來寫就不簡單了。當她解釋的時候，班上興奮的騷動起來。她要我們到黑板前面，一次上去五個學生。她說：「現在寫你的名字。」然後大家就寫下自己的名字。這很簡單。「現在再寫一次，但這次寫的時候，你的左腳要抬起來畫圈。」我們試著做的時候，沒有人能成功。我們邊笑邊開心的尖叫著。輪到我的時候，我也沒寫成功，但是很好玩。昨天很好玩，今天也很好玩，但我還是希望我不用參加夏令營。

生字表

disappointed [ˏdɪsə`pɔɪntɪd] adj. 失望的
c'mon = come on 快點
stir [stɝ] n. 騷動
delight [dɪ`laɪt] n. 愉快

7月10日

今天晚上，趁媽媽跟彼得不在旁邊的時候，我跟爸爸說我不喜歡夏令營。我不敢直接跟他說我要退出，所以我就跟他說我有多痛苦。爸爸看起來很關心的樣子。他問：「怎麼了？」我就跟他說我真的覺得很難受。我說：「我不會英文，所以我總是在犯錯。我一直很緊張，擔心會做錯事。我很討厭自己搞不懂全班在幹嘛，只有我一個人老是搞錯。」爸爸很同情的點點頭。我跟他說更難的是，班上的同學看起來都長得差不多，我分不出來誰是誰。爸爸很驚訝。他問：「真的嗎？」還睜亮了眼，以為我在開玩笑。我很怕他會笑，但他沒有。「拜託，爸，」我求他，「我真的很痛苦。我只認得坐在我兩邊的同學。」爸爸非常的諒解，他說他會處理。他真是世界上最棒的爸爸，沒人像他一樣了解我。

生字表

come out　直接說出
miserable [`mɪz(ə)rəbḷ] adj. 悲慘的
concerned [kən`sɝnd] adj. 擔心的
sympathetically [ˌsɪmpə`θɛtɪkḷɪ] adv. 同情的
sparkle [`spɑrkḷ] vi 閃亮
plead [plid] vi. 懇求
suffer [`sʌfɚ] vi. 受苦

7月11日

媽媽是個樹迷，今天她帶我和彼得到沙加緬度，只為了去看樹。爸爸沒空，所以我們得搭公車去。沙加緬度是加州的首都，州政府大樓旁邊種了各種各樣的樹，每棵樹都有一個標籤寫著樹的名字，還有它的來源地。自從媽媽聽說有這些樹之後，她就一直想要看看它們。吃完早餐後，我們三個在公車站等開往沙加緬度的公車。我們坐了一個多小時才到。到的時候，媽媽把一張地圖拿出來對照街上的路標。我們沒來過沙加緬度，感覺上像是在未知地帶的探險家。街上有些人看起來也很怪。還好州政府大樓就在附近。媽媽很愛這裡，我們慢慢的繞著這個區域走，媽媽很仔細的看了看每棵樹。她說：「它們真是漂亮。」接著我們在附近的餐廳吃了點東西，然後就回家了。我不像媽媽對樹那麼著迷，但到一個陌生的城鎮去很令人興奮。

生字表

capital [ˋkæpətl̩] n. 首都
label [ˋlebl̩] n. 標籤
explorer [ɪkˋsplorɚ] n. 探險家
unknown [ʌnˋnon] adj. 未知的

7月 12日

今天爸爸說我們要去另一種超市。彼得問：「它們不是都一樣嗎？」爸爸說：「不是，這家超市不一樣。你可以在這裡找到許多其他店沒有的東西，而且你們兩個今天還要練習用美金呢！」我們一進店裡的時候，我就注意到空氣中有種特別的香味，聞起來非常的棒，讓我覺得很舒服，但架子上的食物看起來都是一樣的。這個香味是哪裡來的呢？爸爸給我們一人五塊錢，然後說我們可以買自己要的東西。這五塊錢都是用銅板湊的！我們得算出正確的價錢。我在走道上逛來逛去，最後發現香味的來源，原來是新鮮的咖啡豆散發出來的。媽媽和爸爸都是愛喝咖啡的人，他們喜歡喝直接由咖啡豆做成的濃咖啡。如果咖啡加了奶精和糖我就喝，但媽媽說我加那些污染的東西會毀了好咖啡。

生字表

aroma [ə`romə] n. 香味
figure out 算出
aisle [aɪl] n. 走道

7月13日

媽媽早上叫我起來去夏令營的時候，我覺得有點驚訝。我猜爸爸還沒跟她提過吧。然後，吃完午餐不久，爸爸出現在我們的教室。看到他我很驚訝。我想：「終於，我痛苦的日子結束了！」我確定他是來帶我走的。「鐵鏽」跟爸爸握了手，而且交談了幾分鐘，然後「鐵鏽」轉身向全班宣布：「好，各位同學，黛安的爸爸帶了照相機來幫我們全班照相。」所有的小孩都高興的嘰嘰喳喳說起話來，有些人還轉頭對我微笑。「鐵鏽」給每人發了張大卡片。他給每人一個號碼，要我們把它寫在卡片上。他說：「要好好寫清楚。」然後他轉頭對我說：「黛安，妳坐在中間。」我坐下，其他女生坐在我兩邊，男生則在後面站一排。爸爸說：「現在把卡片放在下巴下面，然後笑一個！」後來爸爸謝謝我們就走了，可是他沒有把我帶走。怎麼回事？他忘記了嗎？

生字表

show up　出現
buzz [bʌz] vi. 嘰嘰喳喳的說話
distribute [dɪ`stribjʊt] vt. 分發
assign [ə`saɪn] vt. 指定，分派

7月14日

現在是盛夏，白天會變得很熱，有時候氣溫會高達三十八度。每天天空都晴朗無雲，我好喜歡喔！陽光總是讓我覺得很快樂。我去游泳的時候，我喜歡太陽把我手臂跟腿的水曬乾的感覺。每天夏令營下課後我都會游泳，於是我就變得越來越黑。媽媽說我曬得太黑了。前幾天，有位女士走過來用奇怪的語言跟我說了一些話。她看到我的黑頭髮跟黑皮膚，以為我是墨西哥人，就跟我講西班牙文。媽媽覺得很好笑，她說：「如果有非洲人開始和妳說話，我就不再讓妳游泳了。」媽媽喜歡開玩笑。我說：「如果這樣的話，我就在晚上游泳。」其實，我喜歡在晚上游泳，感覺很特別。有些夜晚，星星似乎被困在水裡了，我慢慢滑下水，在星星中間游動。浮在水上的時候，我仰望天空，覺得我跟它們好像合為一體，在太空裡進行自己孤獨的旅程。只有我和星星。

生字表

float [flot] vt. 漂浮
journey [`dʒɝnɪ] n. 旅程

7月15日

今天我們正準備要去游泳池的時候，爸爸又出現了。他帶來了那天拍的照片，每人一張，外加一張給「鐵鏽」。那時我才了解拍照的原因。班級合照都是在學期末才拍，不是學期初拍。這表示爸爸要讓我退出夏令營。今天是我在這裡的最後一天，照片是拍來做紀念的。「鐵鏽」要我把照片發給每一個人。同學們都很開心，那張照片對他們來說是個驚喜，而且他們不用付錢。爸爸說：「我不能留下來，我要趕回去上班了。」爸爸開車離開時跟我們揮手，所有的孩子都大聲揮手說再見。我想我知道為什麼他沒把我帶走了，因為他要我享受最後一天的游泳課。後來，有些孩子走過來跟我說他們多麼喜歡這張班級照：「哇，黛安，妳爸爸好會照相。」至少，我想他們好像是這麼說的，我不確定，甚至也不能確定到底是誰說的。

生字表

drop out　退出

remembrance [rɪ`mɛmbrəns] n. 紀念

7月16日

親愛的莎麗舅媽：

我們到這裡快一個月了，發生了好多事情喔。一開始我們到舊金山的時候住在旅館裡，在市中心的山丘上，非常的漂亮。我很驚訝舊金山的街道竟然這麼陡！我們看到電纜車在山坡上上上下下的走。我們沒有時間去觀光，不過爸爸答應會很快找一天帶我們回去好好的參觀。我很期待那天的到來。現在我們在這個安靜的小鎮安頓下來了。爸爸說這是個「大學城」，因為有個不錯的大學在這裡。他說在美國這種小鎮已經很少了。我們租了一間有游泳池的漂亮房子，它的四周有大樹圍繞著，附近有一個公園。彼得跟我參加了夏令營。說實在的，前兩個星期真的很難熬。我還不是很習慣，而且希望能退出。其他小朋友都很好，只是他們都只說英文。媽媽、爸爸、彼得跟我都很好。請代我們向大家說聲「嗨！」

愛妳的，
黛安

生字表

cable car 電纜車
sightseeing [ˋsaɪt,siɪŋ] n. 觀光
except [ɪkˋsɛpt] conj. 除了，要不是

7月17日

今天晚上當爸爸跟我說：「我有個新消息要跟妳說。」的時候，我好興奮。這一定就是我一直在等待的消息了。當他說：「以後妳不用再擔心認不出妳的同學了。」我高興的拍手。這真是天下最好的消息。在我的幻想中，我已經可以看到自己在剩下的夏日裡，躺在游泳池旁邊，磨練我的泳技，曬得更黑的樣子。有那麼一下子，我覺得有點罪惡感。「鐵鏞」怎麼辦？「當你跟鐵鏞說我要退出時，他有沒有說什麼？」畢竟「鐵鏞」對我那麼好，他會怎麼想？爸爸露出驚訝的表情：「退出？誰說要退出？」我的心開始往下沉。爸爸說：「我不是告訴妳我會處理這件事嗎？好了，我解決了，來。」他邊說邊給我一張紙。上面是全班同學的名單，以及他們在照片上的號碼。爸爸說：「這是我從鐵鏞那裡拿到的，吃完晚飯後就開始好好看一看吧！晚上十點開始第一次考試。」

生字表

glee [gli] n. 快樂
guilty [`gɪltɪ] adj. 內疚的

7月18日

吃完早餐後，我們跟媽媽去「農夫市場」。「農夫市場」是露天的，在一個公園舉辦。它們一星期才辦兩天。在有市集的日子，附近農村的農夫會帶他們的農產品來這裡賣。媽媽說所有的水果跟蔬菜品質都很好。有很多人在買東西。媽媽買了一些蔬菜，她說價錢非常合理。那裡也有個男的在賣水晶。我從來沒看過天然水晶，我覺得它們很吸引人。那個人跟我說這些水晶已經存在幾千年了，是從阿肯色州來的。當我站在那裡看，想著如果我有一個的話會有多好的時候，媽媽走過來了。她說：「天啊，這些水晶真漂亮。」她一定看到了我渴望的眼神。她說：「妳不用說，我知道了。」現在，正當我在床上寫日記時，我的新水晶正擺在我旁邊，我一看到它就很開心。

生字表

surrounding [sə`raʊndɪŋ] adj. 周圍的
quality [`kwɑlətɪ] n. 品質
reasonable [`riznəbḷ] adj. 合理的
crystal [`krɪstḷ] n. 水晶
fascinating [`fæsṇ͵etɪŋ] adj. 迷人的
longing [`lɔŋɪŋ] n. 渴望

7月 19日

這個小鎮是圍繞著一所大學而建的。每次我們開車出去，在來回的路上，我們都會經過大學的校園。每次我都很努力的往裡面看，可是很難看得到。就好像人家給你一個用盒子裝的禮物，但你還不可以把它打開，所以你會努力猜裡面有什麼東西一樣。我想所有的小孩都知道這種感覺。我們每次經過這個大學時我都會這麼覺得。今天我們又經過那裡，這次一定是第一百零八次了。我再也受不了了，所以我就問爸爸說：「是不是每個人都可以去校園參觀呢？」爸爸說可以。「那你怎麼不帶我們去呢？我很想去看一看。」爸爸笑著說：「有耐心一點，我是把最好的東西留到最後。何況我現在太忙，再過一兩個禮拜，我會放一天假，我保證那時候就去。」彼得嘟噥著說：「大學有什麼好看的。」爸爸笑著說：「你會很驚訝的，彼得。你會喜歡它的。」爸爸總是叫我們要有耐心，可是我討厭等待，特別是會讓人驚喜的事。

生字表

grumble [ˋgrʌmbḷ] vi. 咕噥；發牢騷

7月20日

爸爸叫我把學英文的過程視為一條路，要到達目的地，就必須一步一步的前進，沒有捷徑。他說對我而言，第一步就是要先知道班上同學的名字。現在，我全部都知道了。在這三個禮拜以來，我今天第一次覺得有自信，但這可是得來不易的。昨晚爸爸又考我一次，我還是考得不好。吃完晚飯後，爸爸說：「不可以看電視。」所以我回房間去盯著照片看，但還是沒有用。一個鐘頭後我出來，還是只能認出四分之一的同學。爸爸說：「妳沒有注意看。別只是看這個人的眼睛，然後再看另一個人的下巴，也別管他們穿什麼衣服。妳一定要看整張臉。這就像是學中文字一樣，妳不要光看一角或一劃；妳要整個的看。如果妳把臉當做文字，就不會有什麼困難了。」真有效。現在我不但知道班上每個小孩的名字，我連他們在照片裡的號碼都記得。

生字表

destination [ˌdɛstəˋneʃən] n. 目的地
shortcut [ˋʃɔrtˌkʌt] n. 捷徑
stare [stɛr] vi. 盯
jaw [dʒɔ] n. 下巴
stroke [strok] n. 一劃

7月21日

今天我們玩了一個叫「ZIP/ZAP」的遊戲。這應該是個很簡單的遊戲，可是對我來說卻很難。我們坐下來圍成一個大圓圈，然後「鐵鏽」解釋要怎麼玩這個遊戲。我幾乎可以聽懂所有他說的話，但我還是很緊張。「鐵鏽」跟我們說當「鬼」的人要說「ZIP」或「ZAP」。如果「鬼」說「ZIP」然後指著你的時候，你要說出坐在你右邊的人的名字。如果「鬼」說「ZAP」，你要說出坐在你左邊的人的名字。說錯名字的人就得當「鬼」。我不太擔心，因為現在我知道所有同學的名字了。開始的時候，「鐵鏽」叫我先當「鬼」。他說：「只要說『ZIP』或『ZAP』，然後指一個人。」但當我試著說「ZIP」時，發出的聲音不太對。一開始，全班都笑了，但他們看到我真的有困難的時候，他們就停了下來。「鐵鏽」試著幫忙，可是卻沒用，我就是無法正確的發音。晚上的時候我問爸爸，他說「Z」對中國人來說是個很難發的音。爸爸「ZIP」和「ZAP」的發音都很完美。

7 月 22 日

今天是游泳日。現在我知道班上同學的名字，游泳日就變得越來越好玩了。上禮拜我還分不出來誰是誰，不過現在不會了。今天蜜雪兒、南西、可琳、安崔雅和我潛下水去找一個二十五分的硬幣。會有一個人把硬幣丟進水裡，我們就仔細看硬幣落在底下的哪個地方，然後跳下去看誰先拿到硬幣。好好玩噢！要在水裡找一枚銀幣並不簡單。起先我們用一分，但南西說一分太容易就看得到，她要換成二十五分，所以我們就換了。這幾個女生都比我高大，她們跳下水的時候，總是比我先拿到硬幣。有一次，蜜雪兒已經撿到了硬幣，但她要上來的時候，硬幣從她手裡掉下去。我正好在她下面，所以就接到了硬幣。可琳和安崔雅想要從我手裡把硬幣拿走，於是我們又拉又扯的衝出水面大笑。如果能天天游泳多好。不知道今天晚上，其他幾個女生會不會像我一樣這麼累？

生字表

tug [tʌg] vi. 用力拉

7月23日

夏令營開始的第一天早上，當全班大聲說：「嗨，黛安！」的時候，我覺得那是出自內心的友善。雖然說他們好像有點躲著我，但其實所有的同學都很好。我跟媽媽提起這件事。她說：「嗯，妳站在他們的立場想想看，如果有個不會說國語的陌生人，來到妳們臺北的學校，妳會有什麼感覺呢？就算妳想跟他做朋友也沒辦法。他們只是不知道該跟妳說什麼而已。」沒錯，我同意媽媽說的話，但我開始發現班上有一個人真的對我很不友善。我不知道他是誰，但好像是其中一個男生。班上玩遊戲的時候，我有時候會弄不清楚狀況並犯錯。老師們都很有耐心，其他同學也一樣；但我發現當有這種情況發生時，會有一個人咕噥著說一些不太友善的話。每次都是同一個聲音。今天，「鐵鏽」叫他不要再這麼做了。我不敢看他是誰。我實在不想知道他是誰。

生字表

genuine [`dʒɛnjuɪn] adj. 由衷的
mention [`mɛnʃən] vt. 提到
mumble [`mʌmbl̩] vt. 咕噥著說

7月24日

對於認得賽門這張臉，我一向都沒有問題，甚至在夏令營剛開始的日子裡，在我知道每個人的名字之前，我就認得出賽門。他比其他的孩子都高大，而且他也是個欺負弱小的人。我不知道其他同學覺得怎麼樣，但是我不喜歡他。只要我們有美勞課，瑪拉幾乎都會讚美賽門的作品，有時她會在全班面前把它舉高，讓大家欣賞。今天瑪拉給我們看了一些野生動物的圖片，她要我們選一種動物來畫。我選了豹。後來，瑪拉說我的畫是全班最好的。我不知道瑪拉是真心這麼說，還是只是想試著鼓勵我，反正，這種感覺很好。她叫我站起來到前面，讓全班看我的畫。其他同學看起來都很佩服我，甚至有些同學看起來真的在欣賞我的豹，不過賽門可沒有。他就坐在那裡，看起來一臉不高興。我可以在他眼中看到憤怒。就因為一張畫嗎？真令人難以相信。我最好離他遠一點。

生字表

bully [`bʊlɪ] n. 惡霸
admire [əd`maɪr] vt. 欣賞
leopard [`lɛpɚd] n. 豹
respectful [rɪ`spɛktfəl] adj. 尊敬人的
sullen [`sʌlɪn] adj. 不高興的
stay clear of 避開

7月25日

今天早上貨運公司打電話來。我們從臺灣託運過來的家具到了，星期一就會運來我們家。我們都很興奮。媽媽打電話到爸爸公司跟他說這個消息，爸爸說他那天會請假，這樣我們可以馬上把房子整理好。他不想等到週末。我問爸爸我和彼得是不是星期一也可以留在家裡，但是他說不用了，「你們從夏令營回來後有的是時間。」晚上吃晚餐時，我們討論哪些東西要放在哪個房間。其實，我們在搬進來的時候就討論過了，但那是在我們房子還很新、很陌生的時候說的；現在既然東西真的到了，我們要再重新計畫。做計畫是很有趣的。現在我坐在床上，試著想像我要怎麼佈置自己的房間。說也奇怪，我其實不太清楚媽媽幫我打包了什麼東西。唉，這不重要了。我覺得有特別的事情會發生。真等不及了。

生字表

plenty [ˋplɛntɪ] n. 大量

7月26日

今天下午，爸爸在市中心的書店閒逛，我跟彼得覺得很無聊。我們問爸爸可不可以走到火車站那裡，他說：「去吧，可是半個鐘頭之內要回來。」我們剛來到小鎮時，就住在火車站後面的旅館，不過我們從來沒有機會去火車站那邊。彼得說：「我們去瞧一瞧，看看是什麼樣的人在坐火車，一定會很有趣。」所以我們就去了。火車站很小，沒有很多人在等車，但是他們都看起來很開心的樣子。我猜他們在想著他們的旅程吧！我們遠遠的聽到火車鳴笛的響音，我跟彼得趕快跑出去看 。 一個又美又亮的火車頭慢慢的停靠在車站邊，在車頭後面是一長列的客車車廂。彼得驚訝的說：「哇！看起來好新噢！看起來很棒吧！」當大家上車後，火車就開動了。列車長跟我們揮手，我們也向他揮手。火車看起來又光亮又有氣勢，如果我也能搭上那班火車多好。

生字表

browse [brauz] vi. 瀏覽
horn [hɔrn] n. 警笛，喇叭
exclaim [ɪk`sklem] vi.（由於興奮、痛苦或憤怒等而）呼喊
pull away （運輸工具）開始起動
conductor [kən`dʌktɚ] n. 車掌
sleek [slik] adj. 油亮時髦的

7月27日

當我從夏令營回來時，家門口停了一部大卡車。我們從臺灣運來的家具到了！卡車司機跟他的幫手卸下所有的東西，並且幫我們搬到房子裡。他們問東西要放在哪些房間，我們跟他們說把所有的東西都放在客廳裡就好。我們很急切的把箱子打開。這就像是跟熟悉的老朋友再見面一樣，我的私人寶藏都在裡面。我把它們集合起來收到我的房間，跟我的水晶及其他東西放在一起。媽媽裝運來了她最愛的椅子及黑檀木桌子。媽媽喜歡木器，她第一次在一家古董店看到這些東西時，就對它們一見鐘情了。爸爸運來了他的書架和他的藏書。「書能成家」是他最喜歡的格言之一。媽媽看著這些東西說：「嗯，要把這些東西歸位會是一件苦差事。」但是她是笑著說這句話的，我們都知道她很高興。今天是又忙又快樂的一天。

生字表

unload [ʌn`lod] vt. 卸貨
antique [æn`tik] n. 古董

7月28日

嗯，我想我今天發現誰不喜歡我了。今天早上我來上課的時候，賽門站在門外面。如果我早點看到他的話，我就會避開他，但那時候已經太遲了。我往門口走去的時候，他用他兇惡的小眼睛瞪著我；我給他一個平常的微笑，但他卻哼了一聲轉過頭去。我確定他就是每次在我犯錯的時候，一直在那裡唸唸有詞的那個人。賽門跟別組一些年紀比較大的男生站在一起，當他們看到他不理會我的招呼時，全都大笑了起來。我不覺得他只是因為瑪拉讚美我的畫就生氣，我想他可能從一開始就不喜歡我。瑪拉的讚美只是讓事情更糟。我本來一直都不想知道是哪位同學不喜歡我，我以為也許等我學會一點英文之後，不管是誰，他會慢慢的改變想法。唉，現在太遲了。如果他想跟我說什麼話，我就笑著假裝我聽不懂。

生字表

mean [min] adj. 卑鄙的，兇狠的
snort [snɔrt] vt. 輕蔑地哼著鼻子
remark [rɪˋmɑrk] n. 言詞，談論
ignore [ɪgˋnor] vt. 忽視，不理會
upset [ʌpˋsɛt] adj. 不高興的
worse [wɝs] adj. 更糟
dislike [dɪsˋlaɪk] vt. 不喜歡

7 月 29 日

今天發生了一件很奇怪的事。前一秒我還站在游泳池邊，和珊德拉及克萊兒說話，下一秒我就飛在半空中。天空和游泳池顛倒了過來，我重重的栽在水中，浮上來的時候，水嗆得我無法呼吸。我聽到珊德拉生氣的說：「你故意推她的，賽門。我看到了！」賽門一臉無辜的回答：「我才沒有。她一定是自己滑倒的。」我受夠了賽門。我脫口而出：「不，我才沒有。」我的英文突然像河水決堤一樣，源源不絕的冒出來，連我自己都覺得驚訝：「你故意的。你總是在找麻煩，大家都知道。」就像爸爸曾經說過的一樣，我不用思考要說什麼，話就自己跑出來了。大家看著我，全愣住了。我警告他：「你最好別再試著那樣做，不然你會後悔。」賽門用挑戰的口氣回答：「哦，是嗎？」說完，「鐵鏽」就走過來了。他說：「我全都看到了，賽門，離開游泳池。你兩個星期不准游泳。」

生字表

hurtle [ˋhɝtḷ] vi. 猛然衝進
choke [tʃok] vi. 噎住，嗆到
sputter [ˋspʌtɚ] vi. 噴濺（唾液）
innocent [ˋɪnəsṇt] adj. 無辜的
slip [slɪp] vi. 滑倒
break through 決堤
startled [ˋstɑrtḷd] adj. 受驚嚇的
defiantly [dɪˋfaɪəntlɪ] adv. 挑釁的

7月30日

今天早上，瑪拉要我們創造出「奇妙的生物」，她準備了大概三十張不同的野生動物、鳥、甚至一些迪士尼電影卡通動物的圖片。「好了，小朋友。你們每個人要創造出自己的奇妙生物。我要你們用自己的想像力，不要抄旁邊小朋友的。」有些小孩子看起來很無助，不知道要畫什麼，不過我可不是這樣。我看了一下在教室另一邊的賽門，他穿著黑色的褲子、白色襯衫，襯衫上有粉紅色的條紋。我埋頭開始畫了起來。賽門有個回頭看人的習慣。我先畫一個大野狼狡猾的回頭看的樣子，就像賽門平常一樣；然後我幫它畫了個男孩的身體，讓它穿上跟賽門一樣的黑褲子和襯衫。最後，我畫了一條長長的老鼠尾巴從後面伸出來。之後，當大家把畫拿給全班看的時候，全班都開心的大嚷大叫。他們很清楚我畫的是誰。

生字表

creature [ˋkritʃɚ] n. 生物
stripe [straɪp] n. 條紋
slyly [slaɪlɪ] adj. 狡猾的，不懷好意的
stick out　突出，伸出

7月31日

今天克萊兒和梅蘭妮跟我一起走回家，她們跟我住在同一個方向。她們以前從來沒有邀我跟她們一起走過。說實話，我之前也不想跟她們走，因為那時我幾乎不會說英文，對她們和對我來說，那樣會很尷尬的。所以她們走在街道的一邊，而我走在另一邊；如果我們的視線碰在一起，我們會微笑著說「嗨」，但大多數的時間她們會假裝沒看到我。我覺得無所謂。畢竟，我們能談什麼？我們沒有共同的話題。但是今天，一切都變了，好像班上每個小朋友都過來跟我說話。嗯，其實也不是每個人。賽門當然沒有跟我說話，他連看都不看我。經過昨天的「奇妙的生物」練習，其他小朋友發現我很幽默，而且他們都很喜歡我這一點。爸爸說幽默是某種語言，所有孩子都能了解，不管你是那裡來的。我從來沒有這樣想過。

生字表

awkward [ˋɔkwɚd] adj. 尷尬的

sense [sɛns] n. 感官、意識

8月1日

在大學商場有家賣甜甜圈的店，每次我們去商場裡的市場時，店裡總是有很多人坐在那裡，喝著咖啡或茶並吃著甜甜圈，但我們從來沒有進去過。今天買完東西後，爸爸和媽媽決定帶我們去吃吃看。看到老闆居然是中國人，我覺得很驚訝。我們每個人都點了一個甜甜圈，媽媽和爸爸還點了咖啡。當我咬下我的甜甜圈時，我敢說這是我吃過最好吃的甜甜圈！老闆過來幫我們倒咖啡，他問我們是從那裡來的。爸爸告訴他我們是臺灣來的。他和藹的笑著用國語說：「我也是臺灣來的。」他坐下來跟我們聊了一會兒。他說：「我兒子在大學裡工作，所以我就開這家店來打發時間。」當我們準備要走的時候，他堅持要請客。後來，爸爸說這個老闆人很好，但我唯一想著的是最快什麼時候可以再來吃甜甜圈。

生字表

donut [`do,nʌt] n. 甜甜圈
swear [swɛr] vt. 發誓
chat [tʃæt] vi. 閒聊
insist [ɪn`sɪst] vi. 堅持
on the house　免費的

8月2日

我從來沒有注意到我們後面那一棟兩層樓的房子。它隱藏在一棵大樹後面，幾乎是看不到的。今天，我坐在我們游泳池旁做白日夢的時候，一隻鳥從大樹上飛下來。我很好奇的看牠在做什麼。牠在我們的草坪上跳來跳去一會兒，很高興的在那裡找尋食物，看樣子牠的收穫不錯。然後我忽然想到：「我的天！牠在吃蟲子！」真噁心！我要怎麼回到房子裡呢？我沒有帶拖鞋過來。想到要赤腳走過我們的草坪，還要壓死幾百萬隻蟲子，我就覺得恐怖。我正在想要怎麼辦時，那隻鳥又飛回樹上去了。我試著再看看牠，但牠不見了，已經消失在樹葉間。透過葉子的縫隙我看到有東西閃動了一下。我再仔細看了看，這時候我才注意到那個窗子。是不是有人在那裡看我？還是在看我們的游泳池？我想著：「會是什麼人呢？」

生字表

invisible [ɪn`vɪzəbl̩] adj. 看不見的
worm [wɝm] n. 蟲
squash [skwɑʃ] vt. 壓扁

8月3日

親愛的黛安：

謝謝妳的來信。聽到妳在剛開始的時候過得不開心，真替妳感到難過。事情一定會好轉的。我相信妳已經渡過了最困難的時刻。當妳看到這封信時，我敢說妳一定開始覺得好玩了。舊金山一定是個很棒的城市。我從來沒去過那裡。黛安，妳真是幸運，我真希望我是妳！我真懷疑自己是否還會有時間再去旅行。現在我有個夢想，如果事情順利的話，也許明年我可以跟妳舅舅去看妳們。妳看，連上了年紀的人都有他們小小的夢想，去看妳們就是我的夢想。我好羨慕妳們住在一棟有樹的大房子裡，還有，妳們甚至有自己的游泳池！聽起來好到不像是真的。對了，妳的朋友茱莉前幾天打電話來，她要了妳的地址。她說她會把地址傳給妳的朋友，所以妳收到很多信的時候可不要覺得意外喔！大家都想多了解你們的新生活。請常常寫信給我們。

愛妳的，
莎麗舅媽

生字表

be bound to　一定
work out　有好結果，發展順利
pass on　傳遞

6月
7月
8月
9月

8月4日

今天，我告訴彼得我看到後面那棟房子有動靜。彼得問我，「妳認為有人在看妳？現在想起來，我從來沒看過有人在那裡。」彼得不說話，靜靜的想了一下。「我們過去看一下好了。」我問他：「你是說翻過我們後面的籬笆嗎？」「不是的，笨蛋！那太明顯了。我們只要走到那條街上從外面看就好了。」我們走出去的時候，彼得數著我們這條街的房子，一直數到街尾。有七棟。然後我們在街角轉彎，往前數我們後面那條街的房子。第七棟是一間白色的兩層樓房子，在它的前院有一個「待售」的大招牌。我認出來「售」這個字是因為有一次在買東西的時候，媽媽指出來給我看。這棟房子死氣沉沉的，窗戶裡都沒有什麼動靜。不知道為什麼，這棟房子看起來有點恐怖。彼得說：「我們快點走吧。」我們就趕緊回到自己街道的安全範圍。

生字表

obvious [ˋɑbvɪəs] adj. 明顯的
threatening [ˋθrɛtnɪŋ] adj. 險惡的

8月5日

今天的游泳課特別棒，因為我不用擔心賽門。他還要再等一星期，「鐵鏞」才會讓他游泳。我真的好愛游泳。媽媽說我上輩子一定是條魚。媽媽的話讓我思考了起來：如果每個人都有上輩子，不知道賽門是什麼？一定是某種很可怕的東西。也許是一條蛇；不只是蛇，而且是條毒蛇；或者他是隻猴子？上星期我看了電視上關於印度猴子的影片，我覺得它們老是跳來跳去，推來推去。它們的行為讓我想起賽門。可能這種想法不太好，這對蛇和猴子來說是種侮辱。我試著把賽門想成別種動物，但似乎沒有一種是合適的。他鐵定不是獅子，獅子是很威武勇猛的。嗯，其實這不重要了。他住在同一個小鎮上，而我們還參加相同的夏令營。賽門是個討厭鬼，但是連他都沒辦法破壞游泳帶給我的快樂。

生字表

poisonous [ˋpɔɪznəs] adj. 有毒的
insult [ˋɪnsʌlt] n. 污辱
fierce [fɪrs] adj. 兇猛的
pest [pɛst] n. 討厭的人
spoil [spɔɪl] v. 破壞

8月6日

今天早上吃早餐的時候，爸爸說：「快要開學了，該給你們兩個孩子買腳踏車了。」我和彼得都很驚訝。學校走路就可以到了，我們從來沒想過爸爸會讓我們騎腳踏車。今天在夏令營的時候，我一直想到擁有自己的腳踏車這件事。我不夠專心，而且犯了比平常多的錯誤，結果我大部分時間都一直當「鬼」。但我不介意。唯一的困難是我不會騎腳踏車。彼得比我好一點，但也好不到哪裡去。在臺北騎腳踏車太危險了，所以我們都沒有機會學騎腳踏車。我們剛搬來的時候，看到好多人騎腳踏車，覺得很驚訝。不只是小孩，連大學生和大人都在騎。這個小鎮是設計給大家騎腳踏車的，在擁擠一點的街上都有特別的腳踏車線道。原因很簡單－騎腳踏車有助於維持空氣清新，而且對身體有益。好像每個人都有一部腳踏車，而現在我也快變成其中之一了。

生字表

bike [baɪk] n. 腳踏車
concentrate [`kɑnsn̩ˌtret] vi. 專心
wind up　結束，結果變成
lane [len] n. 車道

8月7日

吃完晚飯後，爸爸提議我們出去散步，我們都歡呼起來。太陽下山後，冷空氣從舊金山灣吹入山谷裡，晚上很涼爽、很舒服。街上一個人也沒有。我們在月光下散步時，媽媽深深的吸了一口氣。她說：「這不是很棒嗎？我們在臺北永遠都不可能享受這種空氣！」媽媽說得沒錯。這裡的空氣好像不一樣，特別是這裡的夜晚有種香味，不知道是哪種植物散發出來的，但是每次我們晚上出來散步的時候，我都會注意到這個香味。在公園裡，月亮像是低低的掛在樹上，好像如果爬到樹上，伸手就可以把月亮從空中摘下來。我說：「這裡的月亮好大好圓喔。」媽媽說：「妳沒聽過嗎？外國的月亮比較圓。」我們都笑了。在臺灣，這是一個常常聽到的笑話，但是是真的耶，這裡的月亮真的比較大。彼得好像是唯一不欣賞月亮的人。彼得說：「月亮太亮了，它把星星都推開了，它們都被擠到天空的邊邊去了。」媽媽很喜歡這個想法，她說：「彼得，你很有想像力嘛！」彼得的話讓我想到，也許世界上的人不是喜歡月亮，就是喜歡星星。彼得很明顯是喜歡星星的人。我呢，我喜歡月亮。

生字表

fragrance [`fregrəns] n. 香味
hang [hæŋ] vi. 懸掛，吊著
squeeze [skwiz] vt. 擠
imaginative [ɪ`mædʒə,netɪv] adj. 富有想像力的

6月
7月
8月
9月

8月8日

今天早上，爸爸終於帶我們去參觀大學校園了。從我們來到這裡之後，他就已經答應過要帶我們參觀校園，但他一直沒有時間。爸爸到美國念書時就是念這所學校，他常常跟我們說他當年是多麼開心、校園是多麼漂亮。我從來沒想到這校園會這麼漂亮。爸爸帶我們在校園中到處逛，指出不同的建築物給我們看。後來，我們到學生中心去吃午餐，彼得和我吃了披薩。吃過午餐後，我們到外面去，坐在一張被附近樹蔭籠罩著的桌子旁。在他所愛的校園環繞下，爸爸坐著往後一靠就開始講話。他要我們體會他的感受：一個鄉下孩子在二十年前，大老遠從臺灣來到這個寧靜的大學城。他想要我們明白那段經驗對他的意義。他一直說到樹影慢慢變長、附近也沒什麼人的時候為止。我坐在那裡仔細的聽。我永遠都不想忘記他所說的話。

生字表

various [ˋvɛrɪəs] adj. 各式各樣的
shade [ʃed] n. 蔭涼處

8月9日

這是爸爸昨天說的話：「我年輕的時候是個好學生。我不是說我很聰明、甚至喜歡上學；其實我不喜歡上學，但我知道該做什麼，所以我就去做。我的成績一向很好。但老實說，我覺得很多課很無聊，因為老師教得不好。後來我到這裡來，情況就不同了，從我進校園的第一天就感覺得到。我在這裡待了三年，而且享受著每一分每一秒。許多教授都很替人著想也很有耐心，他們不只是教書而已，還指引著我，把我當做是大人，以平等的態度對待我。有時候他們會請我去他們家，因此我認識了他們的太太和孩子。這些年來我跟許多同學還保持連絡，在世界各地有幾十個朋友。但不是每個人都有同樣的感覺。我跟其他不喜歡這裡的學生談過，其中有美國人也有其他國家的人。他們有些人後來就轉學了。但對我來說，在我生命的那個階段，這地方是十全十美的。」

生字表

subject [`sʌbdʒɪkt] n. 科目
present [prɪ`zɛnt] vt. 呈現
professor [prə`fɛsɚ] n. 教授
equal [`ikwəl] n.（地位）相等的人

6月 7月 8月 9月

8月10日

親愛的莎麗舅媽：

謝謝您的來信。您說的沒錯，我開始覺得好玩了。我在夏令營交了一些朋友，也學會了說一點點英文。記不記得我們去年夏天去福隆海水浴場？我那時不會游泳。在這裡的夏令營，我們班每個星期三下午都上游泳課，但是他們不教你怎麼游，因為所有的小朋友早就會游泳了，所以我們就在那裡痛快的玩。剛開始的時候，我覺得壓力好大。上游泳課的第一天，因為我聽不懂老師說什麼，所以就沒帶游泳衣去。真的好糗喔！大家在玩的時候我只能坐在旁邊。我當時就下定決心要學會游泳。每天從夏令營下課回家，我就一直苦練。現在我游得蠻好的，而且我不再怕水了。事實上，我愛死游泳了！下次我們見面的時候，我們可以來比賽。請告訴大家不用擔心，我們開始習慣美國生活了。

愛妳的，
黛安

生字表

pressure [ˋprɛʃɚ] n. 壓力

8月11日

通常從夏令營回家之後，我就馬上到外面的游泳池去，有時候我會游一下子，有時候我就坐在那裡做白日夢。但是這幾天我根本都沒去游泳池。媽媽以為我生病了，堅持要量我的體溫。當然我的體溫是正常的。我怎麼能告訴她我怕後面那扇神祕的窗子？坦白說，我怕的是那棟空房子裡可能會有什麼東西；換句話說，我怕鬼。自從我和彼得發現後面那棟房子是空的以後，我就覺得待在院子裡不舒服。從那天開始，我就想像那棟房子裡可能發生過可怕的事。是不是有人死在裡面？如果從窗戶往外看的那個「人」是個小孩，他是不是在找玩伴？他會不會晚上跑出來，從我們的窗外往裡頭看？我只要一開始想到這些事情，腦子裡就會跳出恐怖的影像。我想我最好關燈上床睡覺。等等，不行，我要開著燈睡。

生字表

normal [ˋnɔrmḷ] adj. 正常的
image [ˋɪmɪdʒ] n. 影像
pop up　突然跳出

8月12日

「鐵鏽」今天提醒我們說還有三個星期夏令營就結束了，也就是說，只剩下三堂游泳課了。他說所有的夏令營在八月二十七號的時候，要集合舉行最後的游泳大賽。雖然我們這個鎮很小，但社區中心開辦了五個夏令營，每個夏令營都在鎮上不同的地方。在我們最後一堂游泳課的時候，每一班要比賽選出最好的選手，而且每一個人都要參加。最好的選手在二十七號會參加夏令營冠軍賽。一想到這個我就覺得緊張，畢竟我是這個暑假才學會游泳的。雖然我有進步，但是想到要比賽我就怕。我不想變成最後一名。我跟「鐵鏽」說我不要參加比賽，他笑著說：「不要擔心！會很好玩的。」今晚我問爸爸那天我可不可以留在家裡，爸爸說：「別擔心！會很好玩的。」我就知道爸爸會這麼說。只是，我本來指望「鐵鏽」會有點同情心的。

生字表

remain [rɪ`men] vi. 剩下
competition [ˌkɑmpə`tɪʃən] n. 競賽
separate [`sɛprɪt] adj. 個別的
race [res] n. 比賽
participate [pɑr`tɪsəˌpet] vi. 參加
compete [kəm`pit] vi. 競爭
championship [`tʃæmpɪənˌʃɪp] n. 冠軍
sympathy [`sɪmpəθɪ] n. 同情

8月13日

媽媽告訴我們泰德叔叔這個星期日要來家裡住。泰德叔叔是爸爸的老朋友，他們從國中時期就認識了。當完兵以後，他們一起到這裡的大學念研究所；爸爸念電機所，泰德叔叔念醫學院的牙醫所。畢業以後，泰德叔叔留在美國，現在在舊金山有他自己的牙科診所。他的太太和兒子會跟他一起來。爸爸和泰德叔叔有好幾年沒見了。我們六月在舊金山的時候，爸爸忙得沒有時間和他聚一聚。晚上吃晚餐的時候，爸爸告訴我們一些他和泰德叔叔年輕的時候做的事情，有些事聽起來真的很瘋狂。爸爸每次講到這些事的時候都會帶著笑容。我不知道將來回憶在夏令營的日子時，我會有和爸爸同樣的感受嗎？我想不會。畢竟，在爸爸和泰德小的時候，可沒有一個賽門出現在他們的生活裡。

生字表

military service 兵役
dentistry [ˋdɛntɪstrɪ] n. 牙科醫學
clinic [ˋklɪnɪk] n. 診所

6月
7月
8月
9月

8月14日

我今天終於鼓起勇氣到游泳池去了。剛開始，我只是把臉貼在對著游泳池的大玻璃窗上往外看。外面的天空很晴朗，一點雲也看不到；樹在陽光下閃耀，樹葉在微風中起舞。我在家裡幾乎可以聽到樹葉發出的沙沙聲。游泳池也是藍色的，就像鏡子一樣反映出藍藍的天空。草皮看起來很軟，像一張青翠綿密的地毯，吸引著我踏上去。我仔細看了看那扇隱密的窗子，它看起來很正常，窗簾都拉上了。我告訴自己，「也許那天我反應過度了。也許那扇窗子後面根本就沒有什麼動靜。」我又等了兩分鐘。外面的誘惑實在太大了，所以我打開了玻璃門。我想：「至少我不要光著腳丫踩死那些蟲子。」我穿了拖鞋就跑，衝過那塊綠色的地毯，不理會那些蟲子死前的尖叫，就跳入游泳池裡。感覺真是太棒了。

生字表

glitter [`glɪtɚ] vi. 閃閃發光
breeze [briz] n. 微風
rustle [`rʌsl̩] vi. 作沙沙聲
reflect [rɪ`flɛkt] vt. 反射
lush [lʌʃ] adj. 青翠茂盛的

8月15日

唉，不管有沒有那扇窗子，我都得努力練習游泳。現在我比較怕變成最後一名，反而不那麼怕是誰在從那扇窗子偷看著我了。今天我不是前後的游，而是橫越池子左右的游，那樣我就不用抬頭，想著是誰站在窗子裡了。晚上吃晚餐的時候，媽媽叫我和彼得明天要好好整理一下房間。她說：「泰德叔叔來的時候，我要房子又整齊又乾淨。」她告訴我們在房間清理好之前不准出去玩。我是無所謂啦，反正我的東西一直都保持整齊，但是彼得就不同了，他有點邋遢。他用完東西以後，總是把它們丟在地上或椅子上。坦白說，他的房間亂七八糟的，他需要東西的時候都找不到，每次都要叫媽媽幫忙找。他說：「喔，媽，他們來的時候我可不可以把門關上就好？這樣就沒人知道我的房間是不是很亂了。」彼得對整理房子的看法可真特別。

生字表

straighten up　整理
sloppy [ˋslɑpɪ] adj. 懶散的
toss [tɔs] vi. 拋，扔

8月16日

今天泰德叔叔、他太太茹碧嬸嬸、跟他們的兒子亞瑟，趕在吃午餐的時候到了。當大人們很開心的在敘舊時，我看了看坐在桌子對面的亞瑟。他比彼得大一歲。泰德叔叔的英文說得很流利，可是我注意到即使在美國待了這麼多年以後，他有些字的發音還是不理想。我注意到這點是因為我在暑假開始時，也有相同的問題。反正，除了亞瑟之外，今天沒有人說太多英文。如果你跟亞瑟說中文，他就用英文回答。吃過午餐後，大人們在聊天時，彼得和我帶亞瑟到公園去。他堅持要一直說英文，可能他覺得我們夏天的時候才來這裡，所以我們的英文應該不太好，而他想要愛現一下。但也有可能他的中文沒有那麼好。我不知道。我現在準備要睡了，而爸爸和泰德叔叔還在聊。

生字表

eye [aɪ] vt. 看
fluently [`fluəntlɪ] adv. 流暢的
show off　炫耀，賣弄

8月17日

今天早上，我聽到泰德叔叔告訴爸爸一個他前陣子讀到的有趣理論：有一個有名的瑞士心理學家容格博士說，不管是什麼種族，人在什麼地方長大就會有那個地方的靈魂。我聽得出來泰德叔叔說的是亞瑟。今天下午，彼得和我帶亞瑟在我們家附近逛逛，但他好像沒什麼興趣。他一直在說舊金山是個多棒的地方。他在說話的時候，我很仔細的看他。如果容格博士的理論是正確的話，亞瑟可能會顯現他那印第安人的靈魂，而開始嗚嗚叫，就像電影裡的印第安人一樣。但最後什麼事都沒有，真是令我失望。當他們準備離開的時候，茹碧嬸嬸說：「快點來看我們喔。」然後他們跟我們揮揮手就走了。當他們的車子消失在街尾時，彼得問說：「爸，我們什麼時候會去舊金山？」看樣子，亞瑟說的大城市生活已經讓他感到興奮了。

生字表

theory [`θiərɪ] n. 理論
psychiatrist [saɪ`kaɪətrɪst] n. 精神病學家
claim [klem] vt. 主張
acquire [ə`kwaɪr] vt. 獲得
soul [sol] n. 靈魂
race [res] n. 種族
reveal [rɪ`vil] vt. 透露
whoop [hup] vi. 高聲吶喊
fire up 使興奮，使感興趣

6月 7月 8月 9月

8月18日

親愛的黛安：

我打電話給妳的舅媽，她給了我妳的地址。妳喜歡妳的新生活嗎？我真羨慕妳可以住在加州。我問我媽說我可不可以到美國去念書，像妳一樣；妳一定可以猜到她的回答是個「不」字。但她說等我長大以後，也許我可以出國念書。說真的，黛安，我想我等不了那麼久耶！我們好像永遠都長不大，妳不覺得嗎？時間過得好慢，尤其是上學的時候特別慢。好像只有在夏天還有放假的時候，時間才過得比較快。美國呢？美國的時間會不會過得快一點？既然我是妳最好的朋友，妳一定要告訴我妳都做了些什麼事。這個夏天，我媽媽替我報名參加英文班。剛開始我不想去，但因為現在妳在美國，讓我覺得跟英文有某種關聯。我很努力學習，但是天啊，英文真難。妳呢？妳現在會說英文了嗎？妳一定要寫信給我喔！不要拖，今天晚上就寫！

妳的朋友，

茱莉

8月19日

今天，「鐵鏽」教我們怎麼做比賽式的跳水。他警告我們：「一定要跳得淺，如果你跳得太深，你會落在後面。」跳水？我不會。我只會頭上腳下的跳水。「鐵鏽」看著我們每個人嘗試做比賽式的跳水。輪到我的時候，我一落水就發出「啪啦」一聲。這並不是比賽式的跳水。我落水的時候肚子先碰到水，這就是小孩子們說的「肚皮啪啦」，而且還蠻痛的。平常有人來個肚皮啪啦，大家都會笑，但今天沒有人笑，大家都很正經。「鐵鏽」過來幫我：「黛安，把身子往前傾，眼睛看著妳的腳，跳水姿勢自然會正確。」我沒有把握，但我照著他的話做，而且成功了！像「鐵鏽」說的一樣。我做了一個完美的跳水。唯一的問題就是，我一跳就直衝到水底去了。「黛安，」「鐵鏽」說，「如果妳比賽的時候跳得那麼深，當妳上來的時候比賽就結束了。」我們又練了三十分鐘比賽式的跳水。只剩下七天就要比賽了。我好緊張喔。

生字表

splat [splæt] n. 飛濺
belly [`bɛlɪ] n. 肚子
flop [flɑp] n. 撲通掉落的聲音
lean [lin] vi. 傾斜

8月20日

夏令營剛開始的時候，瑪拉常常讚美賽門的美術作品，而且每個孩子也都認為他是個不錯的藝術家。我猜想他應該還可以吧！但是現在瑪拉已經讚美我的作品兩次，很明顯的，這讓賽門很不服氣。珊德拉說他找我麻煩是因為他嫉妒我，而克萊兒說這就是他上星期推我下水的原因，不過，我認為這跟美術無關。我認為賽門就是個惹事分子，天生的惡霸。今天我們做了另一個勞作。賽門試著畫我，而且想讓我看起來很可笑。當他把作品舉起來給大家看的時候，瑪拉說：「你要有點新意，賽門。這和黛安上星期做的一樣，只是她做得比你更好。」全班的小朋友都笑了，但他們不是笑那張畫，笑的是賽門。我跟賽門好像在作戰一樣，而到目前為止，他都敗給我了。

生字表

compliment [`kɑmplə,mɛnt] vt. 讚美，恭維
original [ə`rɪdʒənl̩] adj. 有創意的

8月21日

今天下午我和媽媽到購物商場去。我本來希望我們可以再去吃甜甜圈的，但媽媽在趕時間。我們走進去的時候，我們夏令營裡的一些女生騎著腳踏車經過。我很渴望的看著她們的腳踏車。真希望我也有一臺。如果我有車的話，我就可以像其他女生一樣騎著到處逛逛了。她們其中一個看到我，就叫「黛安！」那是坎蒂。其他三個女生是蘇珊、碧翠絲和露意絲，她們都停車和我打招呼。媽媽說：「妳留下來跟妳朋友聊一聊，我馬上回來。」我們談到即將來臨的游泳比賽，猜測著誰是最好的選手。碧翠絲說，在另一個夏令營有一個叫瑞秋的女生，游得非常好。我們站在那裡有說有笑的，直到媽媽回來為止。後來，我們上車以後，媽媽說：「妳知道嗎？我剛才在注意妳，我很驚訝。妳現在真的會講英文了。」現在換我感到驚訝了。媽媽的話讓我想到，我已經好久都沒有擔心英文的事了。

生字表

meet [mit] n. 競賽大會

8月22日

親愛的茱莉：

我好高興接到妳的來信喔！沒錯，我很喜歡我在這裡的新生活，但是我得承認，剛開始的時候我覺得很不好過。我一個英文字都不會講就得去參加夏令營！不過，現在我已經習慣了。對了，我現在會說英文了。我媽媽昨天說我講得不錯耶！妳在信上說妳要知道所有在這裡發生的事。喔，茱莉，事情一大堆，我都不知道要從何說起！我還是先跟妳談談這個地方好了。我們住的小鎮是「大學城」，平常會有幾千個學生在學校上課，但是現在放暑假，這裡變得沒什麼人。我們住的這一帶很安靜又漂亮，我們喜歡在黃昏的時候出去散步。奇怪的是，我們很少看到別人在外面步行。我爸說美國人是戀車狂，沒有車子他們活不下去。這好像是真的。好吧！我該關燈了。我下次再多寫一點。

妳的朋友，
黛安

生字表

admit [əd`mɪt] vi. 承認

8 月 23 日

今天我提醒爸爸要買腳踏車的事，自從他說要買腳踏車以後，我就一直在想這件事。爸爸說他沒有忘記。他說：「其實，我計畫今天去找車。」我以為我們會到商場的腳踏車店去，但是爸爸有不同的想法。他帶我們到大學附近的一家店。爸爸興奮的說：「太好了，他們還在這。」這是一家只賣二手腳踏車的店，爸爸說他在這裡當學生的時候，就是在這家店買腳踏車。我們進去逛了逛。爸爸挑了兩臺給我們小孩一人一臺，然後他又挑了兩臺：一臺給媽媽、一臺給他自己。這四部腳踏車看起來都需要上漆。爸爸說：「東西只要能用，舊的就和新的一樣好。」這就是我老爸。也許這就是為何他喜歡逛舊書店的原因吧！他付了錢之後，我們就把腳踏車放在車上。爸爸說：「我們給它們上點新漆。」我等不及要開始練習了。

生字表

excitement [ɪk`saɪtmənt] n. 興奮

6月 7月 8月 9月

8月24日

我們在五金行的時候，爸爸問我們說：「你們喜歡什麼顏色？」他下不了決定。美國的五金行跟臺灣很不一樣，這裡的店面很寬敞，所有的東西都整齊的排在架子上。家裡維修所需要的東西都可以在這裡找到。從割草機這種大機器到釘子這樣的小東西，全部都在這裡。彼得說：「我要我的腳踏車漆成藍色。」我哀嚎著說：「喔！彼得，那是我想要的顏色。」彼得跟我說：「妳選別的顏色吧！」爸爸跟我說：「沒關係，我們總可以有兩臺藍色的腳踏車。」我說：「我不曉得耶，讓我再看一看好了。」我走在這條放油漆的通道上，咖啡色、藍色、綠色…、粉紅色、紅色…老天，我真不知道要選哪一色。「快點啦，黛安，趕快決定！」彼得開始不耐煩了。天呀，在那種壓力下做決定真難。「靛藍色！」我終於決定了。這是一種很漂亮的藍色。希望爸爸會好好的漆我的腳踏車。

生字表

hardware [ˋhɑrd͵wɛr] n. 五金器具
spacious [ˋspeʃəs] adj. 寬敞的
maintenance [ˋmentənəns] n. 維修
mower [ˋmoɚ] n. 割草機
impatient [ɪmˋpeʃənt] adj. 沒耐心的，不耐煩的
indigo [ˋɪndɪ͵go] n. 靛藍色

8月25日

今天瑪拉教我們怎麼做自己的風箏，大家都很興奮。我小心翼翼的把每個部分拼在一起。但是有些女生就碰到很大的問題，她們怎麼做都做不好。當風箏都做好後，我們就到外面去放。我跑呀跑呀，想讓我的風箏飛起來，最後它終於往上升了。它高高的飛翔在藍色的天空下。很快的，大家的風箏都飛起來了，天空看起來好像擠滿了奇怪的鳥，又俯衝又翻轉的。放風箏的時候，我想到了阿公；他曾經做了一個風箏給我。我們把每張紙剪好，然後把它們黏在一起，阿公還找到了一些細竹枝來做風箏的骨架。他把竹枝拿在小火上烤，這樣竹枝就會彎成他所要的樣子。那是一個又大、顏色又鮮豔的風箏。我們做好的時候，就把它拿到學校操場去放。風箏飛得很高，就像我今天做的這個一樣。在晴朗的藍色天空下，我突然想起了阿公。假如我可以把我今天做的風箏給阿公看，請他跟我一起放，那該有多好。

生字表

soar [sor] vi. 高飛
swoop [swup] vi. 俯衝
frame [frem] n. 骨架，框架
bend [bɛnd] vt. 使彎曲

6月
7月
8月
9月

8月26日

今天我們班比賽游泳，看誰可以參加明天的夏令營游泳大賽。我們女生組先看男生組比賽，看他們比賽的時候，我覺得好緊張。然後就換我們了。當「鐵鏽」說：「比賽者預備……」我們就站到檯子上，準備跳水。哨音一響，我全力往前一躍；我一落水，就拼命游，好跟上大家。一碰到對岸，我就抬頭看了看。克萊兒緊跟在我後面到。太好了！我不是最後一個。但是，怎麼搞的？愛瑪、珊德拉、露比和瓊都接在克萊兒後面到。喔，慘了！不應該是這樣的！我是第二名，僅次於羅麗。羅麗和我要代表班上出賽。我好後悔那麼努力練習！現在已經是凌晨兩點，我還是睡不著。我好累，但是我老想著明天的事。我真後悔我們來到加州。如果我還在臺灣多好。

生字表

take one's mark　各就各位
whistle [ˋhwɪsl̩] n. 哨子
hooray [hʊˋre] int. 好哇！萬歲！

8月27日

早上爬不起太來，但到比賽的時候我就沒事了。比賽哨音一響，我跳下水，使盡全力衝刺到其他人前面。每次我把臉埋在水裡，就可以看見瑞秋的手臂在我右邊划水；她在我前面一點點。我把頭埋在水中，把手臂用力插入水裡。快、快、快！我的肩膀酸痛，肺好像著了火。踢、踢，伸手，多抓水，用力拉。我使勁用力。我什麼都聽不到，只聽到頭在水中才會聽到的那種奇怪空洞的聲音。牆到底在哪裡？忽然我的手碰到了邊。結束了。我抬頭一看，正好看到瑞秋嘩啦嘩啦的游上來了。她抬起頭、臉色蒼白的喘氣。我贏了！我贏她大概有一呎！在場的小朋友又叫又喊的，很多手伸下水池來拉我。我累得爬不上去。就在那時，我看到爸爸，他又跳又叫的替我喝采。他特別請了一天假來看我比賽，而他之前一個字也沒講。

生字表

struggle [ˋstrʌgl̩] vi. 奮力掙扎
with all one's might　用全力
lung [lʌŋ] n. 肺
strain [stren] vi. 使勁
hollow [ˋhɑlo] adj. 空洞的
gasp [gæsp] vi. 上氣不接下氣

8月28日

今天發生了好多事，我要把它全部都寫下來。今天是夏令營的最後一天，營部安排了一個盛大的烤肉會，而且大家都來了；不只是我們小孩子，大家的兄弟姐妹、當然還有所有的父母都來了。然後，就在傍晚的第一顆星星在天上開始閃耀時，夏令營的主任站起來說話了。她就是那位很和氣、第一天帶我跟彼得到教室去的小姐。她說：「在每次的夏令營結束時，我們會頒獎給那些老師認為在夏令營收獲最多的小朋友。」當她開始唸名字的時候，小朋友之間引起了一陣騷動。但我沒有多大的興趣，只想知道克萊兒在那裡。我正在找她的時候，我聽到有人在叫我的名字。有一下子的時間，我很害怕。我做錯了什麼嗎？但大家都看著我微笑，友善的手把我推過人群到前面主任那裡去。主任說：「恭喜妳了，黛安。」然後給我一個刻了字的小獎牌。我不知道要說什麼。大家都在笑，但是他們的笑是溫暖友善的。

生字表

barbecue [ˋbɑrbɪ͵kju] n. 戶外烤肉
award [əˋwɔrd] n. 獎
ripple [ˋrɪpl̩] n. 漣漪
plaque [pleg] n. 徽章

8月28日

(2) 克莱兒跑過來抱住我。她說：「噢，黛安，這真是太棒了！」我還是不知道這個獎牌是做什麼用的。我問她：「克萊兒，上面寫什麼呢？」克萊兒看著獎牌然後唸說：「八到九歲級最佳游泳選手！」最佳游泳選手？我嗎？我真不敢相信！然後「鐵鏽」忽然就站到我們旁邊。他彎下腰問我說：「嘿，這是那個第一天就忘了帶泳衣的女生嗎？」我覺得很不好意思。我告訴他說如果沒有他的話，我是不會成功的。我是說真的。我一定不會成功。他說：「才不是呢，這是妳應得的。妳那麼努力，所以進步那麼多，我真以妳為榮，黛安。」後來，當他轉身準備走的時候，他笑著加了一句話說：「真可惜他們沒有最佳英文進步獎，否則這個獎鐵定也是妳的。」然後他就走了。看著他的背影，我有一種奇怪的感覺。我了解到夏天真的結束了。現在已經很晚了。我寫了這麼多，手都酸了。我的獎牌放在櫃子上，就在水晶旁邊。我忍不住一直盯著它瞧。喔，「鐵鏽」！這都是你的功勞！想想看！我耶！游泳選手！我好愛加州，我永遠都不要走。

生字表

category [ˋkætə͵gorɪ] n. 種類
bend [bɛnd] vi. 彎腰
deserve [dɪˋzɝv] vt. 應得

8月29日

昨天晚上雖然很累，但我躺了很久才睡著。我實在是太高興、太興奮了。早上媽媽叫我的時候，我拖了好久才起來。媽媽今天要去買東西。「下個禮拜就要開學了，妳跟彼得還需要買一些東西。」百貨公司裡到處都掛著牌子，媽媽唸上面的字給我聽：「開學了。」我一直忙著游泳，所以都沒注意到開學的事，但是媽媽注意到了。為了我們開學，她已經準備了好幾天。媽媽買了背包給我們裝書。好像這裡每個人都有一個背包，尤其是大學生。我想要個背包已經想了很久了。後來，我在冰淇淋店碰到雪麗和瑪琳。商場裡多了很多新面孔，暑假不在這裡的小孩子開始回來了。雪麗和瑪琳認識大部分的人，但也有一些人是她們沒見過的。這些人一定是從別的地方搬來的，就跟我不久以前一樣。假期只剩下幾天了。

8月30日

夏令營才結束兩天，但我已經開始懷念它了。沒想到我會這樣，實在是很難相信。剛開始的時候是那麼難受，我還求爸爸讓我退出。那好像是好久以前的事了。最後這個禮拜我希望夏令營永遠不要結束。真不相信六個禮拜已經過去了，不知道再過六個禮拜我還會有什麼感覺。我現在很難過。瑪拉要走了，「鐵鏽」要回到他的大人世界，我永遠都不會再看到他們了。下禮拜開學，又會有新面孔出現，想到這裡我就很擔心。爸爸說不用擔心，但我就是擔心。他說學校只是夏令營的延續而已。他說：「妳已經認識很多人了，我知道妳一定沒問題。」我很想相信他的話，但我沒有把握。不知怎麼的，我覺得從下禮拜開始，我的生活會完全改變。改變對大人來說很容易，就像爸爸一樣，但我現在不覺得那麼像大人。其實我很害怕，就像夏令營開始的時候一樣。今天晚上真的好累好累，真不知道開學以後，我的生活會怎麼樣。

生字表

extension [ɪkˋstɛnʃən] n. 延續

6月 7月 8月 9月

8月31日

爸爸下午打電話回來，這不是什麼稀奇的事，但是媽媽掛了電話之後，看起來像是有心事的樣子。我問她：「媽媽，怎麼回事？」她回答我說：「我也不能確定。」可是我不會這麼容易就被打發走，我追問說：「那妳為什麼看起來那麼擔心？」媽媽回答說：「爸爸的公司剛才通知他說我們不會留下來了。台北的公司需要他，我們得回去。」

我的第一個反應就是鬆了一大口氣；我逃過一劫了。想到去上學我就覺得傷腦筋。我永遠不用再擔心賽門了。回想起來，夏令營相較之下比較容易，尤其是過了第一個禮拜之後。可是上學就完全不一樣了。班上同學比較多，會有許多陌生的面孔；還有，我的閱讀能力不是很好。我是不是說「不是很好」?其實我的閱讀能力很差；是零。一切都要從頭開始，就像一艘降落在外星球的太空船一樣。但是現在我再也不用擔心了。

媽媽是對的。可能我太小還不能體會，但是我並不覺得那麼糟糕呀！可是當爸爸晚上回到家時，我開始有不同的想法了。

生字表

hang up　掛斷電話
put off　把…暫時打發
thrill [θrɪl] n. 心情動盪的感覺
spare [spɛr] v. 解救
dread [drɛd] v. 畏懼

9月1日

彼得在公園跟他的朋友們玩美式足球，在差不多快天黑的時候回到家。當天晚上媽媽告訴他這個消息時，他看起來悶悶不樂的。我知道他是多麼期待能在今年秋天玩美式足球，這個消息等於是終結了他的夢想。可是他一句話也沒說。看得出來彼得比我實際的多了。當爸爸回到家時，彼得的第一句話就是：「爸，我們的東西怎麼辦呢？唉，早知道我們只待這麼短的時間，我們就不用那麼麻煩，花那麼多錢把東西運來了。難道你的公司沒想到嗎？」爸爸看起來比平常還累，他說：「麻煩是我們要面對的，至於費用公司會出。因為公司要送我們回去，他們會支付一切的開銷。」

彼得警覺的問說：「天啊！爸爸，你該不是被炒魷魚了吧？」爸爸回答說：「沒有，其實我升官了。」升官了！聽起來很棒啊！我覺得我好像從監獄被釋放出來了，我實在不懂為什麼他跟媽媽看起來那麼困擾。我說：「這有什麼不好呢？」媽媽說：「妳還太小，所以不用操心這些事，可是這麼快又搬家會有很多不方便的地方。天啊，我們剛剛才習慣了這個地方，可是現在又要搬走了。」

生字表

glum [glʌm] adj. 悶悶不樂的
expense [ɪk`spɛns] n. 損失
sentence [`sɛntəns] n. 刑罰
disctract [dɪ`strækt] v. 心煩意亂的
inconvenience [ˌɪnkən`vinjəns] n. 不便；麻煩

6月
7月
8月
9月

9月2日

今天早上起床的時候，我的興奮感消失了。慢慢的，我開始明白我已經喜歡上這個小鎮。其實，我不只是喜歡它，而是愛上它了。我愛這裡的氣候、安全的街道、和其他許多可以讓小孩子做的事情。慢慢的，我了解到我其實沒那麼想走。

說再見會是一件很困難的事。我們離開臺灣的時候，跟親戚朋友說再見很容易。我們只是離開一年或兩年，所以知道大家一定會再見面的。可是跟我夏令營的朋友說再見是不一樣的，我可能永遠都不會再見到他們了。想到這裡就讓我覺得很難過。

不管怎樣，我一個一個告訴我的朋友，當學校開學的時候，我沒辦法跟他們在一起了。他們問：「黛安，妳要去念私立學校嗎？」我回答說：「不是，我爸爸被調回臺北上班了。」臺灣對他們來說 聽起來很遙遠，他們沒辦法想像任何人會去一個那麼不同的地方。有人問：「難道妳爸爸不能一個人回去嗎？這樣妳、彼得、還有妳媽媽就可以待到明年夏天了。」我必須承認那真是個好意見，可是我知道我爸爸媽媽是絕對不會同意的。

生字表

fade [fed] v. 逐漸消失
transfer [træns`fɝ] v. 調職

9月3日

學校已經開學了，所以我跟我的朋友沒辦法再整天待在一起了。我們不能再像夏天的時候那樣了。我覺得很寂寞。彼得沒說什麼，但我看得出來他寧願待在加州這裡。他可能還想在這裡念完高中呢！仔細想想，每個人在生命的某一個時候，都要自己走自己的路；可是在我們這個小鎮裡，一般說來這件事不到高中畢業是不會發生的。之後，大部分的人就分散到不同的大學，或者是去工作了。可是高中畢業是很久以後的事，我們根本就還沒想過這件事。我想每個地方的小孩都會面臨一樣的命運，可是對我們來說，我們的生活就是現在、就是此時此刻。他們也不想失去朋友。當我看到他們是那麼關心我，我心裡覺得更難過了。在那個時候，我最想要的就是留下來，跟他們一起去上學。我甚至可以忍受賽門、或是任何事，只要我能留下來就好。最近這幾天我真的變了。不管怎麼說，賽門跟我可能根本就不同班，要躲開他會是很容易的事。

生字表

scatter [ˋskætɚ] v. 分散

9月4日

有天晚上吃完晚餐後，我騎著腳踏車在附近的街道晃了晃。再過幾天我們就要走了。晚上已經開始轉涼了，我得穿上毛衣才不會冷。我想再看看我家附近最後一眼。我要確定我永遠不會忘記這個地方。我要跟熟悉的街道還有友善的鄰居說再見。在夜暮逐漸低垂時，房子裡的燈開始亮了，我想像著他們這一刻正在做什麼。有一對老夫妻應該正準備坐下吃晚餐，他們的孩子住在另一個城鎮。我在克萊兒家對面的街上停了下來。然後我騎著車一個接著一個經過所有住在我家附近朋友的家。我在每一個人的家對面停留一下。我沒去按門鈴，也沒有叫他們，我只是看一看，然後記住那個地方。我甚至還騎過了公園，去看了游泳池最後一眼。游泳池現在已經上了鎖，變得很安靜。在那裡游泳的感覺像是好久以前的事了。不知道「鐵銹」現在在哪裡，在做什麼事。唉，至少我會再見到茱莉。我一定要寫信給她：「親愛的茱莉，妳一定猜不到發生了什麼事……」可是再想一想，我可能在她收到信以前，就先到了臺灣了。

生字表

dusk [dʌsk] n. 薄暮；幽暗

9月5日

距離出發的時間越來越近了，有很多最後該做的事要完成。有些事情我們可以馬上解決，比方說我們的腳踏車。爸爸把腳踏車送回去給車商，而對方很大方的把腳踏車買回去了。當然，價錢比我們買的時候低。其他的事必須等到最後一刻。搬家公司會在最後一天來打包我們的家具，準備運回去。但是在他們來以前，我們一定要確定所有東西都打包好了，所以我們就一直一直在打包。真是累死了。我發現我們現在的東西比我們來的時候多很多。光是一個夏天我們就買了那麼多東西，真是令人驚訝。當媽媽要把我的泳衣放進其中一個箱子時，我不讓她裝。她問說：「為什麼？妳還有好幾個月才會用到。距離夏天還早的很呢。」我說：「拜託，媽媽。泳衣很小，我可以放在我的手提包包裡。再說，我就是想帶著它，這樣我會覺得好過多了。」這時候爸爸走過來了。「她當然會覺得好過一點！那是黛安的幸運泳衣呢。」老爸真好，他總是這麼了解我。

生字表

dealer [ˋdilɚ] n. 商人
stuff [stʌf] n. 物品
acquire [əˋkwaɪr] v. 取得

9月6日

(1) 唉！就是今天了。我們要走了。彼得把行李箱裝到車上的時候，我跟媽媽去巡了一下所有的房間，確定我們把東西都帶走了，然後最後一次給大門上了鎖，之後我們全都上了車。當我們最後一次開車出來，我跟彼得伸長了脖子，回頭看我們的家。它看起來又黑又靜。也許是我的想像，但是對我來說，那房子看起來很傷心，好像它不想讓我們離開似的。爸爸把房子的鑰匙留給仲介公司。當我們開車經過這些街道時，我開始用不同的眼光來看它們。我不再屬於這裡。我已經變成外人了。有一小部份的我已經離開了。我半期待著看到自己和朋友，無憂無慮的騎著腳踏車穿過街道。我一直想要一輛腳踏車。我想要腳踏車的欲望，比什麼都強烈。可是，就像我所有的朋友還有我的游泳池一樣，腳踏車也必須留下來。臺北沒有地方騎腳踏車。明年夏天來臨時，我一定會很想念我的游泳池。說來很奇妙，我們這麼容易就把東西當成是「我們自己」的了，但其實這棟房子是跟別人租的，所以游泳池實際上是他們的，不是我的。可是它帶給我許多快樂和勝利。在我心裡，它永遠都是我的。

生字表

load [lod] v. 裝載
carefree [ˋkɛr,fri] adj. 無憂無慮的
triumph [ˋtraɪəmf] n. 成功的喜悅

9月6日

(2) 爸爸的朋友強森先生跟他的太太來機場幫我們送行。我們又再一次踏入舊金山機場的乾冷空氣中。強森先生跟爸爸握了手。他說：「大衛，沒想到我們這麼快就要說再見了。」「我也沒想到。」爸爸回答他，臉上帶著譏諷的微笑。強森先生幫我們從路邊的櫃檯辦理行李登機手續。然後我們提了手提行李，一起擠進了機場的大門。我們從臺灣來的那個晚上，我看不出來這個機場有多大。哇！這個地方真大！到處都是準備要飛往地球上不同角落的陌生人。全世界各地都會有人看著鐘、數著時間在等待他們。雖然他們還在舊金山，他們的心早就飛到他們的目的地去了。坐在候機室裡往外一看，我可以看到海灣對面山坡上的燈光。剛才我打開手提包要找東西的時候，我瞄到了我的泳衣。我的眼睛充滿了淚水。我必須很努力才不讓它流下來。

生字表

see off　為…送行
ironic [aɪ`ranɪk] adj. 諷刺的
curb-side [`kɝbsaɪd] n. 路邊
carry-on [`kærɪˏan] adj. 可隨身攜帶的
globe [glob] n. 地球
lounge [laundʒ] n.（機場的）候機室

6月 7月 8月 9月

9月6日

(3) 終於坐上了飛機。機艙門剛「砰」的一聲關了。我們還在舊金山，但我可以感覺到，臺灣已經透過黑夜向我伸出雙手，越靠越近了。感覺上好像我的心已經跑到前面、超越了某種無形的線。然後，一個很大的隆隆聲伴隨著一陣加速，我們的飛機升空了、盤旋著。柏克萊的燈光還有東灣慢慢的在我們下面沉下去了。當我往後看時，可以看到在山的後面，中央山谷越來越黑的夜色裡泛著微弱的光暈。我的朋友克萊兒、梅蘭妮、還有其他的朋友都在那裡。一直到幾個鐘頭以前，我也住在那裡。不知道克萊兒、碧翠絲、露比、和其他人現在在幹嘛？可能做完功課，準備睡覺了。不知道哪天傍晚，他們會不會也停在我家門口想念我，就像我想念他們一樣？我很想相信他們會，但是不會。他們的生活不會有什麼改變。明天他們會起床、上學、騎他們的腳踏車、做他們的功課。如果他們會記得我的話，那一定是記得我有好幾次給賽門難看的事。

飛機在天空轉了彎，星星在我們頭上，我們要回家了。

生字表

thump [θʌmp] n. 砰的聲音
surge [sɝdʒ] n. 激增
haze [hez] n. 薄霧

index
生字索引

T

U

V

W

愛閱雙語叢書

給愛兒的二十封信
Letters to My Son

簡　宛著

簡宛・石廷・Dr. Jane Vella 譯

杜曉西 繪

中英雙語，附CD

二十篇母子間的心靈對談
二十封溫馨感人的書信

本書集結二十封作者給兒子的家書，作者以風趣流暢的筆觸，取代傳統說教方式，字裡行間盡是母親對兒子的關愛之情及殷殷期盼。這本溫馨且充滿母愛的中英對照書信集，為成千上萬的父母與青少年提供了最佳的溝通管道，也是最好的「悅讀」及學習英文的方式。

愛閱雙語叢書

世界故事集系列

你想知道，
如何用簡單的英文，
說出一個個耳熟能詳的故事嗎？

本系列改編自世界各國民間故事，
讓你體驗以另一種語言呈現
你所熟知的故事。

Jonathan Augustine 著
Machi Takagi 繪

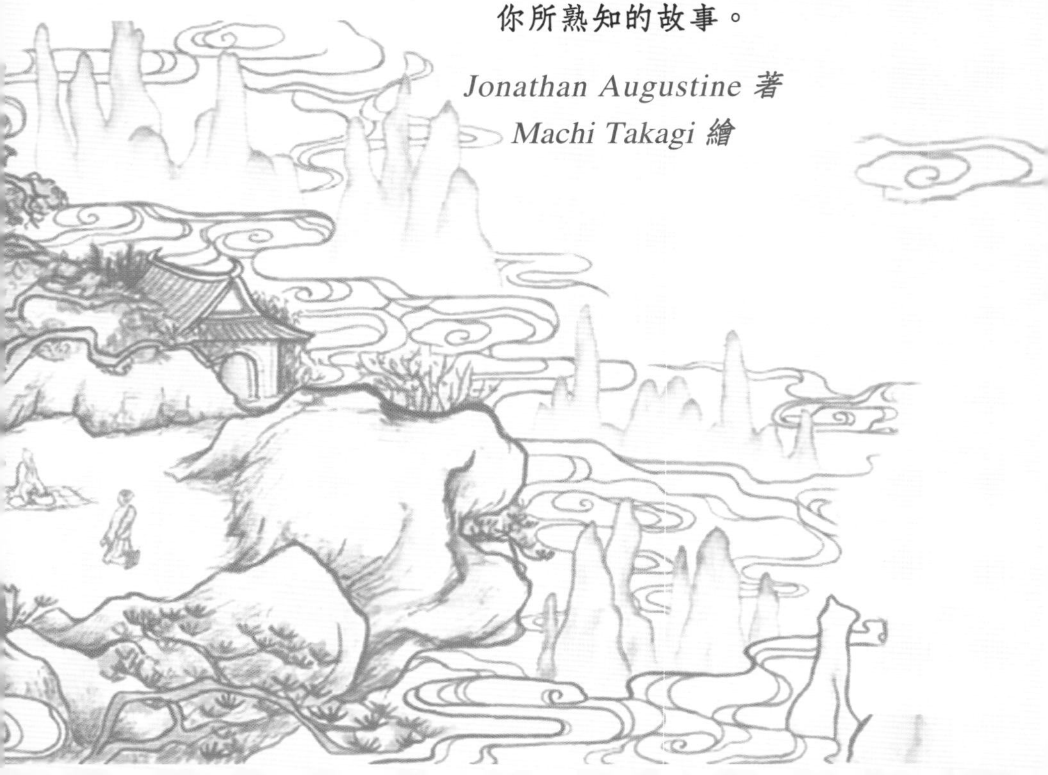

本書改編自中國名著《聊齋誌異》中的短篇故事「嶗山道士」。出生富貴人家的飛龍，因為對仙術充滿好奇，千里迢迢上真山拜一老人為師。時間一天天過去，眼見自己一直重複挑水砍柴的工作，卻不見老人傳授自己仙術，飛龍漸漸失去耐心；同時飛龍又親眼目睹老人在眾多賓客前施展仙術，飛龍決定……

The Land of the Immortals
仙人之谷

如果全世界的人，包括你的家人，在一夜之間全消失了，你會怎麼辦？大衛在被家人責罵後的晚上，許了這麼一個願望，第二天一覺醒來，發現大家真的都不見了！大衛覺得很開心，可是……

Bedtime Wishes
睡前願望

國家圖書館出版品預行編目資料

Diane's Diary:黛安的日記 / Ronald Brown著;呂亨英譯;劉俊男,莊孝先繪.——增訂二版一刷.——臺北市: 三民, 2005
面; 公分.——(愛閱雙語叢書)
中英對照
ISBN 957-14-4235-6 (平裝)
1. 英國語言-讀本
805.18 94001425

網路書店位址 http://www.sanmin.com.tw

© Diane's Diary
——黛安的日記

著作人 Ronald Brown
譯 著 呂亨英
繪 者 劉俊男 莊孝先
發行人 劉振強
著作財產權人 三民書局股份有限公司
臺北市復興北路386號
發行所 三民書局股份有限公司
地址/臺北市復興北路386號
電話/(02)25006600
郵撥/0009998-5
印刷所 三民書局股份有限公司
門市部 復北店/臺北市復興北路386號
重南店/臺北市重慶南路一段61號
初版一刷 2000年9月
初版二刷 2001年2月
增訂二版一刷 2005年2月
編 號 S 802390
基本定價 伍 元
行政院新聞局登記證局版臺業字第〇二〇〇號

ISBN 957-14-4235-6 (平裝)